CLOSER

THAN YOU

THINK

by JayCee Cherry

JAYCEE CHERRY

ACKNOWLEDGMENTS

First giving honor to God. This novel is dedicated to my baby brother, Marlon L. Cherry. May you continue to celebrate in Heaven, my beloved brother.

GOD'S HEAVEN

God looked around Heaven
And realized he had some extra space.
God saw You were here on Earth
Weary, defeated, with extreme agony on your face.

He sent his workers; his precious angels
To take your pain and sorrow away
On April 15th, God embraced you as you
Accepted your heavenly wings and became
God's angel on that day.

Even though you are surely missed
By your family & friends back on Earth.
God knew his plan and purpose for you
When he lent you to us at birth.

Now's the time we must say goodbye
Until we meet again.
God said, "Welcome to Heaven, my good and
faithful Servant
Where your new life will begin."
Sunrise 10-14-1998   Sunset 04-15-2018

3

JAYCEE CHERRY

PROLOGUE

"Have a safe flight, baby. I love you," my husband proclaims to me as we exit his car at the airport. He decided to drop me off instead of me taking a cab or an Uber.

"Call me as soon as you land," he adds.

"I sure will, baby, and I love you too." I gently kiss him on his lips. He hands me my oversized duffle bag from the backseat. I securely place the heavy bag over my shoulder and enter the airport. I turn to make sure my husband has climbed inside of the car and drove off before I decide to reach for my cell phone. When my husband has completely vanished from my view, I call my boyfriend.

"Hey, baby, I'm here. Where are you?" I ask after he answers his phone. Derrick, my boyfriend, is by far one of the best things to ever happen to me. We have been in this secret affair for almost three years, and I enjoy every minute spent with him. He is everything I want in Michael, my husband. Do not

7

get me wrong, Michael is a great husband to me, but there is something about Derrick. He is charming, romantic, extremely funny, confident, and protective.

"I'm about to pull up now baby. Where are you?" There is an unmistakable enthusiasm in his baritone voice.

"I'm waiting by the double doors in front of American Airlines."

I anxiously wait for him to pull up. After two minutes or so, his driver pulls in front of the airport. I can sense he's smiling from behind the tinted glass. I am head over heels for him. Everything about him makes me melt. After three years, I still get edgy when I see him. It's like a flutter of electricity running through my body when he's around. I know he feels the same way, I can tell.

Derrick grabs his luggage from his trunk and walks around the car toward me. Damn, this man is so gorgeous. He stands about six-feet-four, defined by the many years spent in the gym and on the football field, and his body is covered with tattoos. His face is slim, but his strong jawline adds to his oval shape. His dimples rest deeply in the center of both cheeks. His light brown eyes compliment his cocoa butter skin tone perfectly. He has on a fitted white tee with gray jogging pants and all white Adidas. Those gray joggers put more emphasis on how well endowed he really is. He quickly approaches me, only to engulf me into his muscular frame. He always greets me like this, and I love it. After lifting me off my feet and gently forcing his tongue down my throat, he grabs my bag so we can proceed inside. We check our bags in, go through security, and patiently wait to board. Michael calls just to make sure everything is okay, I assume. I ignore his call and send him a quick text message informing him I am okay and that it is too loud in the airport for me to talk to him. I plan to turn my cell phone off this weekend so I can enjoy my time with Derrick. My husband is naive and would never think that I could be having an affair. After all, he thinks I am on an emergency business trip for my job. I'm looking forward to this weekend getaway. I know this will be a trip that Derrick and I will never forget. I just didn't know this would be one of our last trips spent together.

ONE

I've been trying to contact my wife all weekend and when she did call back, which was only once, I missed her call. I figured the service is extremely bad where she is, so I didn't overthink too much of the fact that I haven't heard from her. Ashley and I have been married for almost ten years. Our anniversary is coming up next month, and I want to do something extravagant for us. Ashley has constantly reminded me that I'm not romantic or spontaneous enough, but this year I am going to prove to her that I can be everything she wants in a husband.

I met Ashley at a Christmas party at church. I had just moved to the area and was looking for a church home. I happened to stumble into a local Baptist church down the street from the condominium I was living in at the time. I fit right in at the church, almost like God himself sent me there. I'd never seen Ashley around the town until the Christmas party. She came with another member, Kia, who is married to my best friend, Sean. You know the cliché, "It was love at first sight?" Well, the moment I laid eyes on Ashley, I knew she was going to be my wife one day. Although I was not in favor of her flirtatious trait, I wanted her to be mine. Ashley was by far the most beautiful human I'd ever seen. Her hair was a kohl-black, and it plunged over her shoulders. Her personality was cheerful, elegant, demure and infectious. She had a sculpted figure which was twine-thin. Her waist was tapered to compliment her thin frame. Her skin was the color of a smooth bronze. She had full, heart-shaped lips and her eyes, framed by long lashes, were a bright hazel color. She was perfection in the flesh. Afraid to approach her, I asked Kia about her instead. That was when Kia informed that she brought Ashley to the

party just for me. She figured that she and I would hit it off; she was right. By the end of the night, Ashley and I had already exchanged numbers and planned to go to dinner the following weekend.

Our first date was a hit! My anxiety was at an all-time high. Someone once told me if I was too nervous around a woman, then she was not the one for me. I quickly dismissed the thought of her not being the woman God sent to me. Ashley stayed in an apartment complex maybe fifteen miles from my condo. She was a social worker at the local hospital in town, and she was also a therapist. From what she told me, between her patients and the hospital, her schedule was extremely hectic because she was always on call. She was also in school working toward her Ph.D. in social work, which she only had a semester left. She dreamt of starting her own practice one day but, until then, she was content working for the hospital.

I made sure I was dressed to impress. Ashley was very classy, so I knew I needed to match her

13

style or at least attempt to. Ashley and I talked every day and every night leading up to our date. The more I talked to her, the more attracted I became to her. I loved the fact that she was independent, gung-ho, and ambitious. Her ambition inspired me to reactivate my visions that died years ago.

I pulled in front of her apartment, ready to honk the horn, but decided not to. I figured that would have been a turn off for me to do so. Since she had already given me her apartment number, I parked my car, grabbed the dozen roses that I ordered just for her, and met her at her door. I had already sent her a text letting her know that I was outside before I decided to get out of the car. I could tell from her muddled yet impressed expression that she was delighted I was standing at her door. I handed her the dozen roses. She smiled, exposing every pearly white. Her warm embrace was reassurance that she appreciated me. She wanted to put the roses in some water and asked if I wanted to come in while she finished getting dressed.

"What time is our reservations?" she yelled from her kitchen.

"Eight pm," I told her as I continued to admire every part of her body without being a noticeable creep.

Let's just say we never made it to dinner; instead, I ended up eating her for dinner. I tried to be a gentleman, but this woman was fine. I couldn't resist her. It didn't matter how hard I tried. The last thing I wanted was for her to think that all I wanted was sex. I was all in for this relationship, and I didn't want anything or anyone hindering me from pursuing one with her. I wasn't sure if her luring me into her bedroom was planned or not, I didn't care. I left her apartment a satisfied man.

I know you are wondering how did I end up in her bed? Well, she ended up spilling something on her dress and asked if I could help her unzip it. Do you really think I would say no? Her dress was very thin, thin enough to know that she didn't have any undergarments on. I unzipped her dress, exposing her

15

slim back down to the crack of her buttocks. I was right; she didn't have anything underneath on. What I didn't expect was for her to turn, face me, and completely remove her dress. I watched as she seductively removed the transparent dress from her body. She stood completely naked in front of me, waiting for me to make my move. That's exactly what I did. We enjoyed each other until the sun rays peeked heavily through her blinds.

Needless to say, I ended up marrying Ashley a year or so later. We have the type of relationship that everyone swears they are envious of. I have to admit, Ashley and I are made for each other. She is my better half and I am hers. The only difference we consistently fight about is starting a family. I want children; Ashley doesn't want any right away. She wants to finish school, start her practice, and then concentrate on starting a family. I have my own construction business and have approximately twenty employees. I'm willing to compromise by staying home with our kids, until Ashley finishes school. I figure since my company brings in enough income for the both of us, me staying at home shouldn't be an issue. Nevertheless, Ashley said no. My wife continues to take her birth control so that there will not be any mishaps. I should've switched them out with aspirins.

My cell phone vibrates, knocking me completely out of my deep thoughts about Ashley.

"Hello?" I answer quickly. I had my cell phone placed on my lap in hopes that I wouldn't miss any more of Ashley's calls, but it isn't her; it's my best friend, Sean.

"What's going on? You want to go grab something to eat? Kia left to go visit her mom, and I know Ashley's on a business trip. We need to get out of the house." Sean chuckles.

He's right. I've been stuck in the house the last two days, waiting to hear from Ashley.

"You know what, yeah, let's go," I agree.

"You okay? You sound despondent," Sean says.

17

"Yeah, it's just that I haven't heard from Ashley since I dropped her off at the airport. She called me back one time and that was it. I tried to email her, text her, and I sent her a couple of Facebook messages."

"Dude, why don't you just call her instead?"

"Because my calls aren't going through. Her phone goes straight to voicemail," I rebut.

I can tell Sean is thinking, trying to come up with a good reason as to why I haven't heard from my wife.

"Maybe her service is bad. I wouldn't think too much of it. She said she was behind in her schoolwork and the work from her job. Maybe she's stressed trying to catch up with everything. I totally understand if that's the case. Perhaps she just needs some time to herself right now. Don't trip because you are going to drive yourself crazy over nothing."

"You may be right. I just hope she's okay," I admit. I hate that she traveled without me. This is at least the fourth trip that she's gone on by herself for work.

"I know I am. Ashley is a good woman. You have nothing to worry about. Just get dressed, and I will be there in twenty minutes." He disconnects the phone.

I throw on some jeans and a shirt and wait for Sean to pick me up. I decide to give Ashley a call one more time. It goes straight to voicemail. I check her Facebook and notice that she was active five minutes ago. I send another message via Facebook for her to give me a call or a text. I don't understand how she can log on to social media but not return any of my missed messages.

Sean pulls in front of my house and lays on his horn. Sean is ignorant and does not care what anyone thinks of him. He is a free-spirited individual, and that's what I love most about him. Sean is like my brother, blood can't make us any closer. Speaking of my brother, I actually have a fraternal twin brother that I've never seen. My biological mother put my twin and me up for adoption when we were babies, and we were separated at birth. I spent years trying to find him, fifteen years to be exact. When I mentioned this to Sean, he assisted in the quest to find my twin brother. No one had any information on his whereabouts. All I knew about him was that he'd been transferred to at least five different homes while under the age of eighteen. None of his foster parents had any recent pictures, which made it more difficult to locate him. The last picture I'd seen of him was when he was ten.

Sean was able to locate my biological father in Texas. We decided to fly out there so that I could meet him and perhaps get some information about my family's history. I was ecstatic in knowing that I was going to meet my dad, but my dreams were quickly shattered after learning he was deceased.

My biological mother died shortly after I was born. I was advised that she was involved in a hit and run where she died on the scene. So, meeting my mom was out of the question. Sean set up a Facebook account to see if we could possibly find my brother on there. We found nothing. This seemingly endless and intense journey actually brought Sean and me closer. I trust him with everything I have and I know he trusts me. This is one of the reasons why I considered Sean my brother.

"Really, dude? You just gon' lay on your horn like that?" I howl at Sean from my front door.

One of my neighbors' wails from her window for Sean to knock it off before she calls the police. She's an older woman who nags about everything that happens on the block.

"Dude, get yo gay ass in the car. I'm hungry as hell," he yells back to me.

I quickly grab my wallet, keys, and cell phone from the mini table that's near my front door. It's scorching, ninety-eight degrees outside, and I had the audacity to wear jeans. Ashley is my personal weather girl. Before I leave the house every day, she provides me with a weather update. Since she is not here and I've been stuck in my cool 60-degree air-conditioned home, I have no idea what the weather is like.

"Bro, you didn't get the memo? The heat index is at 117. Why the hell you have on jeans?" Sean jokes.

Beads of sweat begin to trickle down my face and back. I've only walked from my front door to his car. What makes matters worse, Sean is in his drop-top convertible, which means no shade. The more he talks about how hot it is, the angrier I become. Sean is dressed in thin summer shorts, a white tank, and some beach flip-flops.

"Yo, could you please shut up! It's hot and you are starting to annoy the hell out of me," I mutter to Sean.

The blistering sun continues to beam down on me, causing me to almost have a heat stroke. Thankfully, after fifteen minutes, we pull into a local diner. I am about four shades darker and heat rashes have begun to surface on my now swarthy skin. I pray this diner has air conditioning.

"Okay, something is up with you. You better start talking. You ain't never been this quiet. What's on your mental?" Sean inquires after we order our food. I ordered a double cheeseburger, fries, and a vanilla shake. Sean ordered the same but instead he asked for a strawberry shake. It isn't uncommon for this place to be extremely crowded. They have the best burgers and shakes in the world. However, today is different; the place is near empty. Maybe because we were the only fools who decided to leave the house. You know it's too hot when no one is at the beach either.

"Do you think Ashley is cheating on me?" I randomly blurt out. I just need someone to tell me that I'm crazy for allowing thoughts like this to take residence in my head. Someone to tell me that my suspicions are just that, suspicions.

"What? Are you really asking me that question? You know damn well that girl ain't cheating on you. This is your second time mentioning this. Why do you suspect she's cheating?"

"I know this may sound crazy, but these random trips she takes doesn't sit well with me," I reply, recalling the many times she would inform me of a business trip either the day before or the day of the trip. Her being on call is the reason she often uses for the late notice.

"So you're basing the fact that she takes random business trips as a reason for her cheating?" he interrogates. He makes it sound more stupid than what it is. I know I'm not feeling an unexplained unease for nothing. I am 100% faithful to Ashley, never stepped outside our marriage, and have never had the desire to. Unfortunately, we live in a society where people have completely repudiated the value of relationships and marriages.

"How do you explain her not answering any of my calls or texts every time she goes out of town? She barely returns my calls, but she can post pictures and update on her social media pages," I snap.

"Well, have you asked her?"

"Yeah, all the time."

"Okay, what does she say?"

"She says she only has access to those who have an iPhone because she's only connected to Wi-Fi when she's out of town. If I had an iPhone, we could FaceTime and send iMessages to each other."

"Okay, that makes sense. Kia and I have iPhones, so I know how that goes. She probably doesn't want to accrue any excessive charges for using her phone while she's roaming. I'm not sure what the problem is. Just buy an iPhone! Besides, I've been telling your whack ass to switch over to Apple. It gets no better than Apple," Sean laughs.

I'm not in the mood for laughter. I just want some answers.

The waiter approaches our table with our food. I'm ready to partake in one of the seven deadly sins—gluttony. I've already convinced myself to take an extra dinner home.

"You never answered my question!" Sean says, swallowing a large amount of his milkshake. I wait for the moment that he grabs his temple in pain from having a brain freeze, but he continues eating.

"What question?"

"Why don't you just buy an iPhone?' Sean replies.

"The iPhone isn't really the issue; it's the fact that her business trips are in the Bahamas, Cabo, Jamaica, and even Italy. She is in the Bahamas as we speak! What social worker travels to places like that for business?"

There's a puzzled look on Sean's face. He's completely inaudible and staring directly at me. I waved my hand to knock him out of his deep trance.

"She told Kia that she was going to Illinois," Sean finally said.

"Illinois? She's in the Bahamas. I saw her plane

ticket. Why in the heck would she not tell Kia the truth? They are best friends!" I hiss, not toward anyone in particular though.

"Yeah, I can see why you are suspicious. I would hope my Kia isn't hiding anything from me to protect Ashley. That would make her just as guilty as your wife."

"What do you think I should do?" I mumble. I really want to give Ashley the benefit of the doubt. She really has no reason to cheat. We have amazing sex. I pretty much do everything she asks of me. I'm a great provider, and I treat her like a queen. You can't get any better than me.

"Pray. Ask God for clarification. He will give you that. Right now, your judgment is clouded. I'm not going to tell you what you should or should not do, but I do think you should brace yourself for the worse."

"The worse? What are you saying? You think she's cheating too, huh?" I hint as I gulp down the last bite of my burger. I've already demolished the fries and pretty much my whole milkshake.

"I'm not going to lie, it sounds like it. My mom always told me, what's done in the dark comes to the light. Nevertheless, she also said if you go looking for something, you are going to find it. So just be prepared if she is cheating. Think about how you are going to handle the situation."

I ponder on that thought all the way back to the house. The heat has completely drained me, and I'm ready to lay down. Sean drops me off but not before telling me to keep my head up and that he loves me.

Inside, I remove my clothes and lay across my bed. I reach for my cell phone and decide to call Ashley again. No answer.

TWO

Ashley

"Hell yeah, suck that dick, baby." Derrick moans as I continue to suck him while massaging my clit. He helps guide my head by grabbing ahold to my hair, while I continue to bob in an up and downward motion. This is probably the only time I've allowed him to grab my ponytail. I love pleasing him and I'm willing to do whatever it takes to make him happy. I abruptly stop sucking his dick to turn my cell phone on vibrate to silence the calls of my husband. I mount Derrick and ride him until he comes inside me. I immediately collapse against his chest, in dire need of some water. I didn't get a chance to climax, but I'm content in knowing he is satisfied. Besides, we've had sex since we landed. I've had more orgasms than Jenna Jameson.

"Who is that?" he asks as I roll to lay next to him.

"Who is what?"

"Who keeps calling your phone?"

"It's my job, baby. I told you I'm training a couple of new people. That's probably them calling to ask questions. They are just going to have to find out on their own," I lie.

Okay, I know what you are thinking. Derrick doesn't know anything about Michael. I never told him I'm married and I don't intend to tell him. Before you start judging me, let me explain. I have certain needs that certain people can fulfill. Derrick fulfills my sexual desires and majority of my personal needs. Whereas Michael, he fulfills the rest; spiritually, provider, financially, etc. I am truly in love with two men. If I could have them both, I would. I know that I'm wrong because Michael loves me, but so does Derrick.

"Didn't you tell them you were on vacation?" Derrick growls.

"Yes, baby, but those new interns don't care, especially when they don't know anything."

Derrick doesn't say anything else. He just lays in silence and stares at the wall. He finally turns to face me, fondling my nipples as he asks, "Why haven't we moved in yet?"

"Because I'm fucking you and my husband!" is what I really want to say but, again, I concoct another lie.

"Because I'm afraid of losing you?" He knows my breasts are my hot spots and if he continues, we'll be making love again very soon.

"Losing me? How would you lose me if we moved in together? That would bring us closer together, don't you think?" He beams at the idea of us living together. He pulls one of my nipples into his mouth and traces his wet tongue around the border of it. In desperate hopes to distract him from the start of an argument, I softly moan hoping to give off the vibe that I'm still in the mood. He completely disregards my attempt and continues to search for his unanswered questions.

"Well?" he asks as he delicately removes my breast from his mouth. I pretend not to hear his question by asking if he is hungry.

"We should try that restaurant near the front of the resort. I hear the jerk chicken is amazing."

Derrick doesn't answer; instead, he gets up from the bed to retrieve his clothes from the floor. I know he is upset, I can tell from the forceful way he grabbed his clothes.

"Why are you so upset?"

Why did I ask that question? Here we go…

"What the fuck do you mean why am I so upset? I've been playing this damn game with you for the last three years! I've asked you at least twice to marry me! I've never been to your fucking house! I've never met your parents! Nothing! I don't know shit about you! Now that I think about it... I must be your side dude! Is that what it is? You fucking with someone else?" he barks. I've never once had the pleasure of seeing this side of him. He is always tender.

"No, it's hard to explain right now. You know I love you more than anything in this world. It's just... my living situation at home is extremely complicated right now. I'm in a situation that's hard for me to just leave," I explain, and I mean every word. I really do love Derrick, but I'm not going to leave my husband.

"I thought you lived alone, Ashley? How complicated can it be?"

"I'm FUCKING MARRIED!" I blurt out. That was not intentional. I'm just tired of lying to him.

"What?" he finally asks after two minutes of processing that information.

"You heard me. I'm married, Derrick." I lower my head into the pillow. Derrick doesn't say a word.

He turns and immediately begins packing his belongings.

"Wait, where are you going? Please don't leave," I plead. I even attempt to grab his arm to direct his attention toward me.

"BITCH! DON'T FUCKING TOUCH ME!" he screams.

I have to think of something quick! The man that I love is in the process of walking out of my life for good. Think, Ashley... quick! What can I say to keep him around? Hurry, Ashley! He's getting ready to open the door... THINK!!!!!!

"He beats me! I'm so terrified of leaving him! He may kill me if I leave."

Oh, shit, Ashley! Really? Is this the best you could come up with? I continue to ask myself why, but it's enough for him to not walk out the door. I know you may think I'm selfish, but so what; I am. That's the exact reason I don't want any kids. To be honest, I'm surprised I'm still in my marriage.

Michael always says I'm inconsiderate and selfish.

Derrick stands facing the door, with his back toward me. He doesn't move. I know he is pondering on what I revealed. I just hope he turns around and comes back to me. I whisper the words, "I'm sorry," so he can hear. He finally drops his two bags from his shoulders and comes back inside. He shuts the door and walks over toward me. I don't know why I feel the need to break down, but I think it would add an amazing ending to this dramatic scene. I only wish there was a director off to the side to say, "And scene," to conclude it all.

"Why didn't you come clean about this before? You could've been honest with me from the start," Derrick mumbles into my ear.

"I had no idea I was going to fall in love with you. I wanted to tell you, but I was afraid for your safety and for mine," I lie. I wail uncontrollably against his chest. He doesn't wrap his arms around me, but at least he allows me to rest my moist face against his Prada shirt.

"My safety? What has he been doing to you?" Derrick scold.

Uh oh! What have I gotten myself into? I've completely forgotten about Derrick's past. He used to be a notorious thug and drug dealer. He has at least six or seven bodies on him—meaning he murdered them—that I know of. I can hear in his voice that I may have crossed the wrong line. I, in no way shape or form, want to get my husband involved in my mess.

"Nothing major, just threats for the most part. I'm just scared to leave him."

"You said he beats you! You didn't say shit about fucking threats. Has he put his hands on you?"

Fuck it, I can't lose Derrick. "Yes, a couple of times!" I lie again.

"Have you gone to the police?" he asks.

"No. Too afraid to." I cry hysterically, like a newborn ready for his afternoon feeding. Derrick finally wraps his strong arms around my small frame to ensure that everything is going to be okay.

"We are going to fix this, Ashley, don't worry about anything," he says as he places his head on top of mine. I continue to hold on to him, not wanting to break this moment. Even though what I am doing is dishonest, I can't find it in myself to tell him the truth.

"What's your husband's name?"

Before I can even think about it, I yell out, "Michael." I quickly try to recant and give him an alias name of "Tyree" but it's too late. Derrick does not buy it for one second that my husband's name was Tyree.

"What are you planning to do to him?" I attempt to challenge Derrick into spilling the beans but it doesn't work. I silently pray that Derrick will not do anything bizarre. I should have just told the truth and let Derrick walk out of my life. What was I thinking? I wonder if I really love Michael. There is no way I could if I'm doing all of this just to keep my boyfriend around.

"Let me handle all of that," he says. Derrick grabs my chin to lift my head. He looks directly at me and asks, "Do you want me to get rid of him?"

My mind tries to process the words, "rid of him". By "rid of him", does he mean kill him? Alternatively, does he mean scare or pay my husband off to leave me? Either or, my husband isn't a punk by any means. So scaring my husband off isn't going to work. All of this would be so simple if I just tell the truth, right? I'm in too deep. Telling the truth could ruin the chance of Derrick and me ever being together. I should be more concerned about Michael's and my future, I know. However, there's just something about Derrick I can't shake off.

THREE

If my wife, Kia, ever cheats on me, I will probably kill her. I mean it. There are very few faithful husbands left. Kia and Ashley are two of the lucky ones to have married them. Michael gives everything he possibly can in his marriage. I hate seeing my boy down about the possibility of infidelity in his marriage. Michael is a good man, God-fearing, provider, protector; the list goes on. Not to sound homosexual, but he is also a very attractive man. The women damn near grovel at his feet when he enters the church or anywhere we go, for that matter. We—Michael, myself—and two of our friends took a trip to Palm Beach a couple of years ago. We didn't make it to the hotel before

39

women were knocking at our doors. These women were absolutely stunning and didn't give a single care about sucking you off if or when you asked them to. There was a huge party happening the first night we were there. People from around the USA came to Palm Beach during Memorial Day weekend. There's no secret as to what goes on down there, which is why our wives were somewhat reluctant about us taking this trip in the first place. Neither Kia nor Ashley had anything to worry about; it was the other two guys who were with us that were up to no good. However, they were single men; they were entitled to do whatever they wanted to.

The party was jumping. Women were naked everywhere, men barbequing, music, tons of dancing and swimming. Just having a good ol' time. If I had to guess, at least 100 women approached Michael within the first hour of us being there at the party. At least seventy-five of them invited him back to their hotel room. Michael, being the faithful husband that he is, declined every one of them. I, on the other hand, wasn't as well-mannered as Michael. I can admit now that I was wrong and vacuous, but I was immature then. I didn't take my wife seriously, and it almost cost me my marriage. After countless months of counseling, Kia and I have been on the same page. I would never cheat on Kia again. I'm surprised she even considered staying with me after what happened.

Kia is amazing, actually she's heaven sent. We've known each other since grade school. I actually dated her my freshman and sophomore year of high school. We broke up shortly after that, but we maintained a close friendship. Kia was the only girl in high school who wasn't sexual active, and I got tired of waiting. There was something about her, something that kept me drawn to her. It wasn't all about sex; I just wanted to be near her, in her presence every day. Even though she and I were not an item anymore, I still asked if I could take her to prom. I was elated after she said yes. I decided not to pressure her about having sex; I mean, she was still a virgin. Besides, I had already planned to hook up with a girl named Lacy after I dropped Kia off after prom. Kia, however, had a different agenda of her own. I wasn't aware of the surprise hotel room her older cousin rented for us after we left the dance. When she asked for us to stop at the Holiday Inn, I was confused. I contemplated whether I should go in. Kia didn't know this, but I was also a virgin. Yes, that's right, I was still a virgin. I had a reputation around high school of being that "man" but the truth of the matter was the only pussy I'd seen was on porn.

I was nervous as hell when I was invited into her hotel room. Even though I had planned to hook up with Lacy, Kia was different. Lacy was a whore; she slept with half of the basketball and football team. I'd actually walked in on her giving two guys from the football team a blow job in the boys' locker room. I knew Lacy was extremely experienced, so I figured she would not notice that I wasn't. Long story short, I didn't sleep with either Kia or Lacy. I couldn't take Kia's virginity, at least not that night. I knew she was only doing it to make me happy, but I assured her that I was never going anywhere and I meant that. I knew

I was going to marry Kia, I just didn't know when. We lost contact after high school and reconnected about six years later. We immediately hit it off. It's safe to say that neither of us were virgins after our reconnection. I married Kia about two years later. Our marriage has been a roller coaster, mostly because of me. Nonetheless, I'm a changed man now. We decided to keep God first in our marriage and learn how to communicate effectively with each other. We still have our disagreements but nothing compares to how they were before. Kia is my rock and I am hers. Unfortunately, we will never be able to expand our family beyond us unless we adopt. Kia was in a terrible car accident, about five years ago which caused severe hemorrhaging. Neither of us knew she was six weeks pregnant. The accident caused her to have a miscarriage that ultimately resorted to a hysterectomy. We were devastated, not only to find out that we had lost our baby, but that we could never bring life into this cruel world again. Even though I was beyond distraught, I was blessed that my wife was alive.

"Hey, baby, what are you doing home so early? I thought for sure you would still be at the grocery store," Kia asks as she walks through the front door. I'm so distracted by the idea of Ashley cheating on Michael that I didn't hear Kia enter.

"I haven't gone yet. I'm going soon. How was your day?" I ask as I follow her into our bedroom.

"Oh my God, I had one patient who came in with a fork embedded in his neck. Thankfully, he survived. Then there was a kid who decided to iron his baby sister's arm. The stuff kids do! It was a hectic day, baby. I'm just glad I'm off the next three days, and I'm not on call either!" she says as she flops backward on the bed. I know she's had a rough day, but I'm curious if she knows anything about Ashley's extramarital affairs.

"Hey, have you talked to Ashley?"

"No, I tried to call her, but she didn't answer. She called me back this morning but I was with a patient, so I missed her call. Why?" Kia sits up to give me her undivided attention.

"Well, Michael said he's been trying to contact her since she left, but he hasn't gotten in touch with her." I sit down beside her on our bed. Kia is so damn fine. Everything about her is sexy. The way she rolls her eyes, the veins in her neck, her perky lips, the way her hair lays completely flat around the top of her neck… just everything. Kia is mixed with African American and Chinese. Her mane is long and curly. Her face is narrow and the color of smooth vanilla. Her high cheekbones rest perfectly beneath her seductive gray eyes. Her full pink lips sit center in the midst of her beauty. She was perfectly made.

"Um, I'm not sure what's going on. Maybe she's just busy with work and all. I'm sure she'll call him soon."

"Where is she?" I query.

"Illinois… for her job. Why are you asking me all these questions, baby?"

"Michael said she's not in Illinois, she's in the

Bahamas!"

"Bahamas? That's not what she told me," Kia says as she gets up to get undressed. For whatever reason, I'm not buying her story. Kia starts fidgeting which makes me wonder if she is lying.

"Kia, you wouldn't lie to me, would you?"

Kia turns and looks me in my eyes as she replies, "Of course not, baby."

I ask her if Ashley is cheating on Michael and she does what normal best friends do—takes up for their girl. I didn't expect Kia to tell me the truth because I wouldn't tell on Michael if he was, but there's nothing wrong with being hopeful.

"Have you ever wanted to cheat on me, Kia? I mean, I've put you through a lot of shit. I've cheated, I've lied... I've done it all. Hell, I deserve it if you ever decide to cheat on me."

Kia doesn't say anything. She leans against our closet door with her matching lace bra and panties. I am serious about what I said. I do deserve it. I don't deserve Kia. Women like her are priceless. Even though it's a continued effort for me to become a better husband for Kia, I can't help but wonder if she's ever stepped outside our marriage.

Kia walks over to the bed where I sit. She grabs me by my hands and tells me she will never betray me. She kisses me on the lips and tells me she's about to hit the shower. I watch as she gets completely undressed. I can still see the scar from the hysterectomy; other than that, Kia's body is flawless. She walks out of the room after telling me she loves me and enters the bathroom where I can hear the faint sounds of running water. I wait until I know she is in the shower. I remove all of my clothes and decide to join her. She greets me with a huge smile and a long, sensual kiss. I make love to my wife, not caring about how scorching hot the shower is. I planned to heat things up in the shower anyway. The way she sucks my dick is nothing short of amazing. I could come right away but I quickly stop her so I can release inside her. I want to feel her tight, warm, wet pussy lips on my dick. I slightly bend her over so I can see her juicy ass bouncing against my lower abs. It doesn't take long for me to reach my climax. I tried to hold out as long as I could but her sex is too good. After I finish, we wash each other down and take a much-needed nap.

FOUR

"Bitch, call me asap." I text Ashley. My husband is sound asleep as I silently creep out of our bed. It's close to six pm, and I want to get dinner started. I need to talk to Ashley before Sean wakes up. Not even two minutes after sending Ashley that text, she calls me. I hurry to the basement so that I won't disturb Sean.

"Girl, next time you decide to tell the truth about where you are, at least inform me so that our stories match," I scold through gritted teeth, trying to get my point across. I'm so pissed at Ashley. I hate being in the middle of her bullshit. I knew Ashley was somewhere being a whore, but that was none of my business. I always remind her how amazing her husband is and to do right by him, but she's a grown ass woman. Even though I love Ashley like a sister, she doesn't deserve a man like Michael.

"What the fuck are you talking about now?" she cautiously snaps, trying to keep her voice down. Derrick must be nearby.

"Sean told me that you told Michael you were in the Bahamas. You told me you were going to Illinois, so that's what I told Sean. They must have been talking for Sean to randomly ask me that question."

"Who are they?" Ashley asks.

"Bitch, our husbands! What is going on, Ashley?"

"Kia, I fucked up, girl. I don't know what to do." She sounds extremely depressed.

"Is everything okay? Where are you?"

"I'm in the Bahamas. I think I just made the worst mistake of my life. I messed up, Kia."

I can't make out if she's starting to cry or were just talking low so Derrick can't hear her; that is if she's with Derrick. You never know with Ashley. This isn't her first affair, and I'm pretty sure it's not going to be her last. I hate that I introduced her to Derrick. Derrick was an old friend of mine from college. We were never intimate but great friends. Derrick didn't last a semester in college. He loved the streets excessively, and he loved fast money. Had I known he and Ashley were going to start an affair, I would have never sent him to Ashley for counseling. I knew he had gone through some things in his past life, and I knew Ashley was a dope ass therapist too. Even though she's getting her Ph.D. in social work, she has her MBA in Psychology. I have to admit, Derrick is fine as hell. If I wasn't in love with Sean, I would've sat on his face. Shit, I couldn't really blame Ashley though. I wanted to sleep with Derrick on many occasions, especially after I found out Sean was a cheater. I took my vows seriously, so I never acted on temptation. I would often imagine Derrick being Sean while we made love.

"What are you talking about? Tell me?" I grimace.

"Wait, hold on," she whispers. Everything goes silent for a second until I hear Derrick asking her a question. I can't make out what is being asked but I hear Ashley respond by saying, "Sure." Honestly, I'm somewhat jealous that Ashley is with Derrick. I've always had a crush on him; I still do to this day. Ashley brags about how great his sex is, and she boasts about how spectacular his head game is too. Please don't get me wrong when I say I love Sean because I truly do, but I understand why Ashley is so crazy over Derrick.

"Kia? You still there?"

"Yeah girl, what is going on?" I demand to know.

"Girl, so, I finally admitted to Derrick that I'm married. He kept asking me why he's never been over my house and why he can only see me certain times of the day, yadda yadda yadda. After I told him, he was about to leave me and I panicked. I lied and told him that Mike beats me and that I'm afraid for my life. I told him that's why I haven't left my husband yet."

"Bitch, you did what? Why the hell would you lie like that? And, I thought you told Derrick about Michael? Besides, you know how Derrick is; he will kill Mike! What the hell were you thinking?"

"That's just it, I wasn't thinking, Kia. I didn't want Derrick walking out the hotel door or out of my life. That's the only thing I could think of to make him stay," Ashley sobs.

This girl is fucking crazier than I thought. What would possess her to say something like this about a man who would actually give his life for her? I want her to stop telling me about this situation because I really don't want any part of this, but I have to admit—this shit is juicier than Jerry Springer.

"Girl, I'm afraid to even ask what Derrick said. I know him."

"He asked if I wanted to get rid of him, Kia, like kill him. He said he was madly in love with me and that he would do anything to keep me safe," Ashley weeps.

At that moment, I realize how badly she's fucked up.

"Ashley, you need to fix it and fix it fast. Derrick will kill Michael and you know this," I plead with her.

"Don't you think I know that! I really don't need you judging me right now, Kia. I'm not perfect like you, okay! Although I try to be, I'm just not!"

"I'm not perfect either, Ashley, but I would never put my husband in harm's way because I can't keep my damn legs closed. You need to get your shit together, leave Derrick the hell alone, and bring your ass back here with your husband! That man loves you, Ashley; he would do anything for you. I can't understand for the life of me why you continue to cheat on him…" I inhale deeply and wait for her to defend her actions when I realize the line is cold. "Hello? Ashley? Ash?..." I repeatedly call her name until I finally hear a dial tone.

"No, this bitch didn't hang up on me!" I whisper. This whole situation seems convoluted. Part of me wants to call Michael and tell him what is going on. He doesn't deserve this. But I remember my momma always telling me not to get involved in other people's messes. However, this mess is totally different and worthy of a head's up. I dial Michael's number and as soon as he answers, I quickly hang up. He calls right back, but I make up a lie saying I was trying to call my cousin and apologize. That isn't uncommon for me to do. I disconnect the call, hoping Michael doesn't think twice about me calling his phone. Wrong! My phone quickly vibrates again...

"Michael, you okay?" I ask him. I knew it was a bad idea to call him in the first place, let alone answer the phone when he called back.

"Yeah, but I need to ask you something, Kia. You don't have to answer it if you don't want to. I'll totally understand." He clears his throat before he continues, "First, do you think I'm a good husband?" Mike weakly mumbles, and my heart instantly begins to break.

"I think you are a damn good husband, why do you ask?" I ask, even though I know where this is going.

"No reason in particular," he responds.

"Mike, there's something I need to tell you," I attempt to hurry with what Ashley told me, but I'm quickly interrupted as Sean screams who I'm talking to.

"It's Michael, baby, I called him on accident. I was trying to call my cousin to check on him," I yell from the bottom of the stairs.

"Tell him to call me right quick," Sean yells back.

"I heard him, Kia. I'll give him a call," Michael says, saving me the breath to repeat what my husband asked of him.

"What is it that you wanted to tell me?" he reminds me.

I have to quickly make up a lie. There is no way I'm going to snitch on my girl, at least not right now. However, if I find out that Derrick is planning to kill him then I'm singing like Jennifer Hudson.

"Nothing, just wanted to see if you could help me throw a surprise birthday party for Sean in November? I want to have his parents and siblings here for the celebration." Now my ass has to throw a party that I never intended to throw because I can't mind my damn business.

"Oh, that'll be dope. I'll be glad to help out," he says with extreme excitement.

We said our I love you's and Goodbyes and disconnect the call. I swear when Ashley brings her ass home, I'm going to slap the hell out of her.

FIVE

I can't understand why Ashley has been lying to me all these years. As much shit as we've been through, her being married was the last thing on my mind. However, it all makes sense now; her random pop-ups, her disappearing after seven pm acts, her abrupt ending to our phone calls, etc. I probably should've never started sleeping with my therapist in the first place. The only reason I decided to give her another chance after she broke the news about her being married is because she has a couple of my kilos stashed at her house. I can't risk her snitching out of anger; I'll be incarcerated for the next twenty-five years minimum. I want to reach out to Kia and ask if she knew Ashley was married and if she did, why she didn't tell me. Wait! Of course, that bitch Kia knew; they're best friends! I plan to say something to her when she picks Ashley up from the airport. She should've warned me once I told her I was falling in love with Ash.

I didn't have any intentions of sleeping with Ashley. She was my therapist for almost a year before anything happened. Even though she was absolutely stunning, she was a great listener. Every session with her gave me hope for something better. She made me see the value in myself that I was never able to see. During one of our many sessions, things got extremely heated. It wasn't a scheduled session, but I called to see if she had any openings that evening. I really needed to talk to someone because I was ready to blow my cousin's head off. He was short $30,000 of my drug money, and I was already on probation. I knew Ashley could talk some sense into me. When she told me she had an hour to spare and I could come into her office, I quickly showered and got dressed.

When I arrived, Ashley was looking good as hell. She had just gotten her faux locs done. The blonde streaks in her locs complimented her beautiful caramel skin tone. She had on a sexy black dress with heels that helped define the muscles that rested in her calves. Her dress was cut low, giving off the illusion that she was braless. I was completely speechless when I walked inside. I couldn't take my eyes off her. She finally asked me to sit on the couch near her chair, but my dick had something else planned. I knew I was about to cross the line, but I was willing to take a chance. Before she was able to sit in her chair next to the couch, I pulled her close to me. I leaned in for a kiss but was quickly reminded that I crossed the line with a hard slap to the left side of my face. I was stunned to know that much power came from a woman so petite. I grabbed my face, trying to ease the pain; I almost slapped her back until she placed her small, frail hand on the side of my face. She pulled me close to her, this time taking the lead. We shared a passionate kiss before she pushed me down on the couch behind me. She straddled me as I unzipped her dress. She removed the straps one by one from her shoulders, exposing her small but full breasts. I gently massaged them, taking each firm nipple into my mouth, as she slowly ground on my lap. I was completely hard. I lifted her up so I could lay her down on the couch. I helped remove her dress and her soaked thong. I admired every inch of her body. She was flawless, not a stretch mark in sight. It even looked as if she had just gotten a fresh wax. She spread her legs by draping one leg over the top of the couch, giving me a better view of what I couldn't take my eyes off of. I wanted to taste her, hoping it would taste as good as it looked. I dove right in, massaging her pussy with my tongue. She climaxed immediately. I removed my shirt and pants while I watched her masturbate to keep herself moist. I was silently praying that I didn't come quick, plus, I didn't have any protection. The moment I slid inside her tight walls, I knew it wouldn't be long before I released. I was right; five minutes didn't go by before I was clenching my teeth. She understood as she held me closely on her chest. We rested there for about an hour before I finally got up. The rest was history. We made love every time we saw each other. I felt sorry for the people who came in and out of her office because we graced every inch of it. I wined and dined her, exposing her to the finer things that life could offer. I quickly fell in love with Ashley. I knew I wanted to marry her after about six months of dating. She was everything I thought I wanted in a wife. But there was something secretive about her, and now I know. She was married the whole time. I ignored a lot because I hustled every day, and that's only because Ashley wasn't always around. I was willing to give up the street life for her. I had enough money to start my own businesses so I was planning to do that anyway soon. I was also working toward obtaining my realtor license. I even gave up all of my women for her, even my main chick, Keisha. Keisha was one of the sexiest women alive and was down for whatever. She's been by my side since we were kids. Keisha's parents abandoned her when she was seven. She moved in with her grandmother who later died when Keisha was nine. She was put in a group home but ended up running away shortly after. I met Keisha when she was thirteen at the candy store. I was fourteen at the time, and I was already selling drugs for my uncle. Well, he wasn't my biological uncle but my street uncle. I couldn't take my eyes of Keisha while I watched her stuff a couple bags of Doritos, Snickers, KitKat's and a Mystic Fruit Punch inside her coat. Not only was I watching her, but the security officer who stood at the door like a soldier in World War II carefully watched her too. Before she was able to walk out of the store, she was greeted by the owner and the officer who quickly removed all stolen items from her coat. She aggressively fought while both men tried to remove the last of the stolen goods from her hands. I quickly ran over and offered to pay for everything she had attempted to steal. I ensured the owner that it wouldn't happen again and that I'd be responsible for her if it did. The owner knew the street creditability I had, even at the tender age of fourteen. He rung up the items and told me it was $10.52. I gave him a fifty-dollar bill and told him to keep the change. I tipped the officer with $50 for not calling the police on her. Keisha was already outside waiting for me to come out. I gave her the bag filled with the paid items.

"Thank you so much. You just don't know how hungry I am," Keisha's soft voice finally spoke.

"Hungry? You don't have any food at your house?"

"House? Boy, I haven't seen the inside of a house in three years," she expressed.

"So where do you sleep?"

"In that car over there" She pointed in the direction of the red car that was parked on the corner of the alley.

"Are you homeless?" I just couldn't believe a girl this beautiful was homeless. I could tell she was roughly around my age. Her underdeveloped breasts concurred what I was thinking. Before she answered my question, my uncle pulled up and motioned me toward the car. He needed me to make a drop right quick, and I actually needed the money. I told Keisha to hold on as I walked towards my uncle's Mercedes Benz. I told him about Keisha's situation and asked if she could stay with us. My uncle wasn't too thrilled about the idea, but after I promised him that I would keep an eye on her, he said it was cool. In addition, I knew he was going to put her on his payroll eventually. She would be a good distraction for us to steal cars and other items to make a profit. Keisha and I were inseparable until the day I told her I wanted to be with Ashley. She was devastated. We had just gotten a condo together a year prior. I did love Keisha, but not the way she loved me or the way I loved Ashley. Keisha cried when I moved out of the condominium I purchased for us. She begged me not to leave and pleaded her case on how much she loved me. My heart was broken into a million pieces because I knew I was walking out on a great woman. Keisha held me down when I didn't have shit. She visited me every day in jail and kept my commissary full. She even tripled the money I had saved before I was thrown into jail. She had all my money, plus extra waiting for me as soon as I got home. Even though she had all these great traits that I looked for in a woman, she wasn't Ashley.

Now here I am, with Ashley, who is married to another man. Keisha would've never lied to me. I gave up a lot for Ashley and for her to break this kind of news to me is enough for me to break her face in. Although I would never hit a woman, Ashley is almost an exception. The only thing that saves her is the fact that she told me her husband is abusing her. I vowed to never put my hands on a woman, especially after seeing my foster dad beat my foster mom so bad, she went into a coma for a week and died. Therefore, when Ash told me that she was married, I immediately became enraged and decided to walk away. Any man that puts his hands on a woman deserves to die, period! I'm going to make sure her husband, Michael, never uses his hands again.

"Baby, you sleep?" Ash asks. We fell asleep

after we tried that new restaurant she mentioned. We were so full we barely made it back to our rooms before we crashed. I couldn't sleep long because I couldn't fathom the idea of someone abusing the woman that I love. So many thoughts ran through my mind of how I'm going to kill him. Since I'm on probation again, I have to move meticulously. I can't bring any attention to myself. It wouldn't be hard to pay one of my workers to handle this little situation, but whole my operation—including my immediate crew—is under close surveillance.

"No, just up thinking. You okay?" I rolled over to face her. I move her closer into my chest so that I can feel her against me.

"Yes, but I don't want you to hurt him. Let me handle him on my own. I'll just leave him and run away with you."

"It's too late, babe. I can't take the fact that someone is hurting the woman that I love. Why are you so afraid of him? I told you I would handle it."

"It's not that I'm afraid of him, I just don't want anyone to get hurt," she confides. I'm becoming more frustrated by the minute. I don't understand how she can take up for him after she told me that he whoops her ass. This whole situation seems fucked up if you ask me.

"Ashley, if you don't want me to handle him then I will have to walk away from this relationship. There's no possible way that I am okay with him still around after you leave him. You don't think he will try to come back and destroy what we have? Once he finds out that you left him for another man, all hell is going to break loose," I state.

She's silent for a couple of minutes before she finally opens her mouth.

"Fine. Do what you have to do then!" she rebuts. I ignored her aggressive behavior.

"You love me, Ash?"

"Of course, I do. More than anything."

"And you wouldn't lie to me, would you?"

"Hell no. I will always be true to you going forward. That's the only thing I couldn't tell you. I've been honest about everything else."

"I love you too and I need for you to trust me, okay? I reassure.

"Okay, baby. I trust you."

SIX

Ashley

I enjoyed my vacation with Derrick, but I'm so ready to get home to my husband. I've been thinking of ways to protect Michael from Derrick. The idea of just ignoring Derrick's calls, messages, etc. came across my mind, but he knows too much about me. He knows where I work, where Kia works; where I go to church, where I grocery shop. There's no way I can avoid Derrick unless Michael and I just move across the country. I wish I could go back to the moment when Derrick was about to walk out of my life. I hate that I put my husband in my mess.

I'm on Facebook while Derrick showers. We have an hour before the shuttle leaves to head to the airport. I notice a couple of missed messages from my husband. I reply and ask if he can pick me up from the airport at five-thirty p.m. My flight is due to land at four pm. I don't want to risk either one of them seeing me with the other. I told Derrick that Kia was picking me up and if he asks why she isn't there when we land, I will make up another lie.

Michael replies immediately saying he will be at the airport at five-thirty pm to pick me up. He also tells me that he wants to talk to me about something serious. Before I can respond, Derrick comes out of the bathroom. He doesn't have on any clothes and the steamy hot water still drips from his body. I have no idea what type of pussy control this man has on me, but I'm immediately wet. I shut my laptop and go over to Derrick so that I can suck him off. He doesn't budge as he watches me pleasure him before he releases in my mouth. I clean the remaining semen that I'm unable to swallow with the towel he has in his hand. He gets dressed as I pack the rest of our belongings. Once we check out from the hotel, we wait until our shuttle arrives. I can't wait to get on the plane to get some rest. I am beyond exhausted. Derrick and I had the time of our lives here. We probably slept for a total of eight hours these last four days.

The shuttle arrives on time, and we're walking into the airport twenty minutes later. It takes us two hours just to get through customs. When we finally board first class, I am beat. Derrick, being the gentleman that he is, lifts both of my legs so that my feet rests on his lap. He removes my shoes and gives me the best foot rub ever. This is one of the reasons I don't want to leave him. Michael would never do this for me.

The flight is a rough one. It storms extremely heavy, almost to the point where the pilot announces that he may do an emergency landing. I pray that he doesn't because I want to get home to Michael as soon as possible. I'm still thinking of ways to protect him from Derrick. *Shit, Ashley! Why are you so stupid? Why didn't you just let this man walk out of your life?* These are the questions I continuously ask myself.

After two and a half hours, our plane finally lands. I'm so glad I told Michael to show up later to pick me up. I'm just praying Derrick doesn't demand to stay with me until he sees I'm safe in "Kia's" car.

"What time is Kia going to be here? Can you ask her if she could drop me off? I'll give her gas money," Derrick petitions as I grab my bag from off the conveyer belt. I try to ignore him as I begin to panic.

"Ashley… you heard me?"

"Oh yeah, I'm sorry. I checked my messages and Kia said she is running about an hour late. How about I give you some money for a cab? I'm okay here." I'm not sure how good of an attempt that was to make him go home but he isn't buying it at all.

"Naw, I'm going to stay here with you. There's no way I'm leaving you here by yourself."

Damn, what am I going to do now? Michael

should be here in about thirty minutes, and I'm pretty sure he has already left the house by now.

"I'll be right back, baby, I need to go to the restroom right quick," I tell Derrick as I hold on to the lower part of my abdomen, pretending to be in pain.

I speed walked to the nearest bathroom so that I can call Kia. *God, please come through for me this one last time.*

"Hey girl, I need your help," I tell Kia after she answers her phone. I don't know how I'm going to get out of this lie.

"What's wrong now?" I can hear the agitation in Kia's voice.

"Can you come get me from the airport? I told Derrick that you were coming, but Mike is actually picking me up. Derrick, thinking that you're picking me up, asked if you could drop him off at home too and he would give you money for gas. When I lied and told him that you were running late, he insisted on staying with me. I can't risk Michael seeing me with Derrick. Michael will be here in thirty minutes. Please, Kia, help me!"

"This is exactly why I've asked you to be honest with me, Ashley. I don't mind helping you out of this jam. Had I known, I wouldn't have accepted to do a double tonight. I'm already here at work. Even if I leave, I'm still an hour and a half away from you."

"Oh my God, girl, what should I do?' As soon as I ask her that question, a call beeps in on the other end. It's Michael.

"Hold on, Kia, this is Michael."

"Hey, baby," I say softly

"Hey, babe. I'm outside. You have your bags already?" he inquires with excitement in his voice. My heart begins to ache. I can't believe the woman that I've become. I really feel like shit right now.

"Actually no, we are still waiting for the bags to be sent down to baggage claim." I lied. I needed to buy some time to think of how I was getting out of this shit.

"Okay, well I'll park the car and come in. I'm pulling into the lot across the street," he insists.

"NO! Wait. Here they come now! I'll be out shortly!" I quickly end his call by clicking back over to Kia. I explain the situation to Kia but she isn't of any help. She suggests I sneak out and leave Derrick, but that will be difficult considering the fact that all my bags are with him.

I end the call with Kia and sit in the bathroom for a few minutes to think. I send Michael a text letting him know that I'm coming. My heart beats faster than Usain Bolt running the 100 meters. I leave the bathroom and walk toward where Derrick is buying a bottle of water. Kia's idea is the best option. I run over to my two bags, grab them, and dart toward the entrance of the airport.

Michael stands outside his car waiting for me. I run over to the car, open the back door, and throw both bags inside. I didn't realize how heavy the bags were until I jump in the front seat of our Mercedes. My whole upper back burns from muscle fatigue. I slump down in the passenger seat in hopes that Derrick won't see me if he happens to come outside.

"Really, Ashley? No hello? No hug, kiss?" Michael asks as he climbs into the car.

"Baby, please just drive off... hurry."

"Ashley, what the hell is going on? And why are you so out of breath?"

I lean over to kiss my husband. I need to shut him up for a second so that I can get my thoughts together. He quickly backs away from me, frowning, while wiping his mouth.

"You taste funny as hell, Ashley."

I quickly remember that I forgot to gargle after I swallowed Derrick. His semen always leaves an aftertaste in my mouth.

"I had peanuts on the plane, baby. I'm sorry."

"Do you want to tell me what's going on with you?" he questions again.

"It was just a terrible flight. I saw one of my patients on the plane, and she talked me to death. She even followed me to the baggage claim area to talk some more. So as soon as she turned her head, I took off running. That's why I hopped in the car so quick. I was trying to get away from that lunatic." I'm becoming an expert at lying.

Michael giggles. He knows how hard it is for me to tell someone no and that I'm not in the mood to talk. It isn't uncommon for me to run away from people when I get tired of talking to them. Sometimes I use him as my accomplice.

"You are something else. Why don't you just tell them you can't talk right now?"

"Because, Michael, that's my job… to listen! I can't just tell them I can't talk."

"So you take off running instead and leave them high and dry? What sense does that make, baby?" he

78

says, laughing.

He does have a point. It's asinine to think that running away is an ideal solution. I'm not sure why I'm even putting any thought behind what he's saying. I mean, I just concocted a whole lie.

"Can we stop and grab something to eat? I hadn't eaten since this morning?" I propose, desperate to change the subject. We have at least another forty-five minutes to go before we make it home and that's contingent on the severity of the traffic.

I know he's annoyed, I can tell from the muddled look plastered across his face.

"Sure, what do you have a taste for? You want something fast, or you want to sit and grab a bite to eat?" he asks with attitude.

I can't stop staring at my husband. When I say God took his time with Michael, he really took his time with Michael. I always ask myself, how did I get so lucky? He is truly one of the best things to ever happen to me. After getting off the plane and trying to escape Derrick, I made a vow to not cheat on my husband again. I just hope I can stay true to that vow.

"We should sit down and eat. Let's grab some burgers from that spot on Highway 56. We can wait it out there until traffic dies down."

Michael drives for another twenty minutes before he pulls into the restaurant. We notice the drive-thru line is extremely long so it's a no-brainer to eat inside, but Michael wants to take it to go. Instead of waiting in the drive-thru, we go in to order our food, which is fine because I have to use the bathroom. I have at least two full bottles of water that I need to release.

After giving Michael my order, I rush into the women's bathroom, almost knocking over a little girl who can't be any older than five. My bladder isn't like it used to be. If I don't enter into the next available stall, I'm going to ride home in a puddle of urine. To make matters worse, I have on white jeans. I ignore the smart-ass comment from the little girl's mom as I quickly slam the bathroom door stall. I barely make it before my bladder near bursts.

I wash my hands but not before I come face to face with the little girl's mom. I apologize and try to explain to her that my bladder was extremely weak, which it is. She clearly doesn't buy my story as she rushes past me to leave the restroom. I come out to see if Michael is still waiting in the restaurant. I don't see him at the register, nor do I see him sitting in our car. Unbeknownst to me, there's a similar vehicle in the parking lot, which made me misidentify our car. While attempting to thoroughly describe my husband's features, I ask the cashier if she saw where he went. She remembers him and tells me that he's already left. Frustrated, I turn to leave, but I'm halted by the shrilling screams of random women and the scattering of all the people in the parking lot. Everything around me happens in slow motion. I watch as a familiar man vastly approach my husband who was sitting in the car. I try to scream out, but my sounds are mute. Shock has kicked in; to the point that I can't even scream to warn my husband that

Derrick is behind him.

I reach for my phone but realize I left it in my car. Derrick and I lock eyes briefly from a distance. I'm completely paralyzed as Derrick and I have a stare down. He blows me a kiss and slowly walks away. Michael's lifeless body is slumped over the steering wheel as the blaring sounds of our car horn echo throughout the air. I feel someone tugging on me, pulling me to the ground.

"Ma'am, get down, he's still shooting!" someone yells. All my senses are active, especially my hearing. I put both hands up to my ears, hoping to ease the vigorous ringing sounds endured from all the yelling and gunfire. Someone is still tugging on my arm, trying to pull me down to safety. I screech for them to let me the hell go!

"Ashhllleeeyyyy…" I wake up to Michael swerving the car, almost crashing into the mailbox that sits at the corner of intersection we're approaching. Michael stops approximately two feet in front of the mailbox after jumping the curb.

"Oh my God, are you okay?" he asks, completely out of breath.

"What just happened?"

"You were dreaming. I tried to wake you up. You woke up screaming, scaring the hell out of me. You almost made me crash!"

Thank God that was a dream, and I'm even more thankful that we didn't crash into anything or anyone. I wipe my forehead and step outside the car, needing some fresh air. A couple of people approach to make sure we're okay.

"Is everyone alright? Do I need to call the police?" an older white lady asks as she approaches my husband.

Michael has just gotten out of the car to check to see if there are any severe damages to the front end of our Benz.

"No, ma'am, we're okay. I must've fallen asleep at the wheel," Michael says as he looks my way, ready to take the fall for me. That's the type of man he is. He'll always look out for me.

"Well, sir, you better let that pretty wife of yours drive the rest of the way. I would hate to see you guys hurt."

"Thank you, ma'am. We will be fine. I sincerely appreciate your concern," Michael expresses.

The older white lady looks over at me and smiles, and I return her friendly gesture. She steps closer and whispers loud enough only for me to hear, "Honey, take the wheel the rest of the way. Men are only good for one thing, and sometimes they struggle in that department too. They can't do shit right," she chuckles.

I can't help but laugh too. I thank her before she hops into her lime green Volkswagen Beetle. Those are the ugliest cars ever invented.

Luckily, traffic is extremely light. This whole incident could've been much worse had we been traveling on the expressway. We could've killed someone, or worst, we've could've died.

"How's the car looking?" I ask Michael as he continues to examine the car like he's a mechanic.

"Everything is fine, just a couple of scratches from when the car jumped the curb. I'll get them fixed sometime this week. Are you okay?"

"Yes, I'm good. Are you okay?"

"Yeah. Let's just get home!"

I notice the immediate shift in his demeanor. I don't know if I said something wrong or if he's just upset about the car. I even offer to pay for the damages, but he doesn't respond. We ride home in silence, never stopping to grab any food. To be honest, I'm not even hungry anymore. I just want to get home and go to sleep.

It feels good to be home, finally. Michael opens the back door and grabs my duffle bags. He walks around to my side, I expect him to open my door; however, he walks right into the house, leaving me with a dumbfounded look on my face.

"What the hell is wrong with you?" I snap as I walked into our home.

"Who the fuck is Derrick, Ashley?"

Oh shit! I'm afraid to answer him because I don't know how much he knows about Derrick or my relationship with him. I'm not sure if he went through my phone while I was asleep or if someone called him with some information about our trip. I know one thing for sure; I'm not going to tell on myself until I find out how much information Michael knows.

"I have no idea what you're talking about, love." I remain as calm as possible.

"Don't play with me, Ashley. You yelled out his name to stop whatever he was doing to you in your dreams. Actually, you yelled out his name at least five times. He has to be someone you personally know!"

"Is this why you have an attitude? Derrick is my client, honey! A crazy ass maniac that I have to convince not to commit suicide or kill someone every time he comes into my office. I dreamt that he was trying to take his own life. That's why I woke up in a panic."

"Why do you even bother dealing with those type of people? What if they snap and try to kill you? Then what?"

"Baby, that's my job. I actually love what I do. I'm not afraid of them. Besides, the orderlies and security are usually watching or near me. I'll be fine."

Michael doesn't say anything else but kisses me on the forehead after telling he's going to order takeout and run me some hot water. I'm glad that argument doesn't escalate because I don't have the energy for it.

SEVEN

"Excuse me, have you seen my wife? You know, the beautiful short lady who was with me earlier? She has braids in her hair?" I ask some stranger who I remember was near us after we got off the plane.

"Oh yes! She grabbed her bags and jetted towards the doors," the short Caucasian man says as he pointed toward the doors that lead outside.

"Thanks." I grab my bags and hurry toward the exit only to see Ashley jump into some man's Benz. Whoever this guy is he expects some sort of greeting from her, but she ignores him by slamming the passenger side door. I back into the near corner so that I can survey the scene without being noticeable.

I want to know who this guy is and where he's going with my woman. Part of me wants to go rip his fucking head off, but I suspect something peculiar after seeing his wedding ring. I'm not sure what words are exchanged while they're in the car, but Ashley leans over to kiss him. That's enough for me to put two and two together. That's her husband. Everything she told me about him is true, she really is afraid of him. So much that she doesn't even want to hug or kiss him in public.

As they drive off, I'm able to catch his license plate number. I have enough information on him to get everything I need to know. I reach into my pocket for my cell phone and call an old friend of mine who is a police officer. Anthony and I used to hustle tough back in the day until he was shot in his back. That bullet almost took his life. I can vividly remember the doctors telling his family that he wouldn't make it. I was there right beside his mother, trying to keep her from fainting when the doctor broke the news. If you didn't believe in Jesus, I'm sure that night would've changed your mind had you been there. All his family and friends were gathered in the waiting room discussing funeral and burial arrangements when a doctor asked his immediate family to come into the room. The rest of us who sat in the waiting area just knew what was wrong; he was dead. My heart was broken. I blamed myself repeatedly for getting him into the game and for not being there to protect him. About ten minutes later, his mother came into the room with the brightest smile on her face and told us that Anthony was awake. We all rejoiced and thanked the man above. We were able to see him, two at a time of course. I was the last to go in. Words weren't exchanged; we just hugged and shook hands. Needless to say, Anthony got his life in order and got back into church. After his intense eighteen months of rehab, he was one hundred percent. He applied to be an officer a couple of months after he completed rehab. He's been serving his community for almost six years now. He and I are still great friends. If he needs anything, I got him and vice versa.

"Ant, what's good, man?" I ask after he answers

his cell phone.

"Shit, just sitting in the car, patrolling the streets. What's good with you?"

"I need a favor."

"What kind of favor?" he replies.

"Wait, you're by yourself, right?" I have to ask him, I don't want him to potentially risk losing his job because he has an asshole of a partner who would snitch on him

"Yeah, what's wrong?"

"I need you to look up a license plate for me. I need his address."

"Dude, you better not be getting into any bullshit! I definitely do not need to be put in the middle of it. I have a family now, and I ne…"

"Ant, it's not like that! Chill, bro!" I say, cutting him off.

"I'm at the airport and some guy left his bag. The

tag has his name and I'm assuming his license plate number. I just want to mail his bag to him, that's it."

Anthony sits quietly for a couple of seconds, probably wondering if I'm lying or not. What help adds to my story is the sounds of airplanes taking off and the whistles of the airport security in the background.

"What's the plate number?"

I give him the license plate number and can instantly hear the clicks of his fingers against the keyboard. I pray that he will give me some good news.

"Yeah, his name is Michael J. Thomas. He lives 12584 West Biggmine Road in Phoenix."

"Okay, cool. I'll get this mailed out to him either tonight or first thing in the morning. I appreciate that."

"It's all good. How you been? How's Ashley?"

"I've been good, can't complain. Ashley is

good. We actually just got back from out of town, that's why I'm at the airport."

"Where is she?"

"Over there yapping her gums away, you know how she is."

Anthony chuckles before concluding our conversation.

"Well alright, I'm going to let you go. I have to get back to work. We definitely need to link up soon. It's been about a month since we hung out."

"You know I'm down for the cause. Let's get together this Saturday. We can hit that new bar downtown!"

"That sounds like a plan. Let's say around nine pm?"

"Alright, see you then. Love you, bro!"

"Love you too. Take care!"

I disconnect the call and store the address he

gave me into the GPS in my cell phone.

Since I don't have a ride home because Ashley lied to me, I call one of my homeboys to pick me up from the airport. I opt out of the Uber idea because I want to ride past Ashley and Mr. Michael's home. I don't need an extra eyewitness just in case Michael's death makes national news. I would have to eventually track the Uber driver down and kill him too. I wait for over an hour before my boy Tommy arrives.

"Yo, what's good? Throw your bags in the back seat!" Tommy suggests as I quickly approach his candy apple red Bentley. Tommy is a flashy son of a bitch, but he is sharp-witted.

"I'm good, man, but I need a favor before we go home. I got you on gas too," I assure.

"Yeah, man, whatever you need. Let me know."

"Ashley told me something this weekend that was mind-boggling. The bitch told me she is married!"

"Wait, your Ashley? Shorty that came by the house last weekend? The one you've been seeing for like forever? The one we went ring shopping fo…"

"Dude, YES!" I finally interject.

Thinking about how she's been living a double life cuts me deep. I planned to propose to Ashley this weekend. I had a special evening planned for us our last night in the Bahamas. I had to notify the resort when Ashley was in the shower to cancel the surprise.

"I hope you left her ass in the Bahamas!" I know that wasn't really a question but more so like a command.

"No, I didn't. She told me her husband beats her ass, that's why she's afraid to leave," I snap.

"Damn, are you serious? She's that afraid of him?" Tommy inquires.

"Yeah, she is. I could tell by the way she didn't want to hug or kiss him when he picked her up from the airport. He stood there looking like an idiot when she brushed past him and got into the car," I reply, reminiscing on the events that just took place.

"You love her?"

"Of course I love her. What kind of question is that?" I blurt.

"Then what do we need to do about her husband? You know I don't tolerate any man putting his hands on a female," Tommy jeers.

"I'm glad you asked that question. My boy Anthony just looked up his license plate and gave me his address. I want to drive by there and scope the area. We need this job to be clean. I don't want anyone hurt but him, and I don't want anyone going down for his murder."

"Now you're speaking my language. Put his address in the GPS," Tommy says with the biggest smile I've ever seen. Killing to him is like crack to a crackhead. The only soft spot he has is for children and women. There isn't any amount of money that could be offered for him to murder either one. Weirdly, I admire that about him.

Tommy blasts Sean Paul from his speakers. He's a full-blooded Jamaican. His mother and father both were born in Kingston. His mother fell ill and later died to lung cancer when he was about ten. His father started using our products and died about fifteen years ago due to an overdose. He didn't have any siblings and learned to survive from the streets.

I relax and admire the scenery on this one-hour drive to Phoenix, when Tommy interjects, "Something isn't sitting right with me. If he's beating her ass, why wouldn't she acknowledge him when he tried to approach her?"

"Huh? What do you mean?"

"I mean, any battered woman will pretty much do whatever it is to keep from getting her ass whooped. Plus, that's embarrassing for him to try to kiss or hug his wife only for her to dismiss him. He would've slapped her as soon as he got in the car."

"Tommy, you're overthinking this. It was clear as day she was frightened."

"I don't know. You may be underthinking this," Tommy rebuts.

"I don't believe under thinking is a word," I joke.

"It is today!" he states while trying to impersonate the comedian, Kevin Hart when he did his tour, Laugh at my Pain.

I ignore his hideous attempt of Kevin Hart's impersonation and continue to think about Ashley. I love that woman more than life itself. I believed her when she told me that she loves me and wants to be with me.

Tommy and I stop at McDonald's near Ashley and Michael's home. We munched on our burgers and salty fries while we sit at the corner near their home. We're about fifty-yards or so from the home, so we're pretty close. We wait until Michael leaves the house and hops in his Benz.

"Follow him, try not to lose him and don't be so obvious," I demand as Tommy starts his 2017 Bentley.

We trail closely behind Michael but not close enough for him to notice us. He stops for gas at a nearby gas station. We pull into the gas station but only to grab some snacks, or at least pretend we're grabbing some snacks. Michael catches a glimpse of the Bentley, but he doesn't utter a single word. I have to admit, her husband is a looker. The women that came in and out of the gas station keep their eyes glued on him. One woman even tries to capture his attention by asking if he can pump her gas. Being the gentleman that he pretends to be, obliges then gets back into his car to leave.

We follow Michael for another twenty miles or so before he stops at his next destination—a Baptist church.

"Oh, fuck that, I'm not going in there! I don't play with God," Tommy jokes.

"We're not going in. Just wait here and see what he's about to do. I just need to know his routine, where he goes and who he hangs with."

Tommy and I sit quietly, anticipating what's to come next. Michael stays inside the church longer than we expected so I direct Tommy to take me home. I've seen enough, and I'm exhausted. This plan will take a couple of days to master. Until then, I will keep my eye on Michael.

EIGHT

"Babe, I think I'm being followed."

"What? By who?" Ashley wonders.

I called Ashley when I noticed a red Bentley following me. It even followed me to the gas station near the house. I tried to get a plate number or at least an excellent description of the person driving the car. I couldn't make out who was in the passenger seat because the windows were heavily tinted, but I did see the dark-skinned brother who was driving the car. He spoke as we passed each other when I was leaving out of the gas station and he was heading in.

"I'm not sure but they are still behind me," I

shoot at her. I am not mad at her but at the thought of possibly being followed.

"You're probably overreacting. Go to the police if you feel you're being followed."

I dismiss Ashley's idea of going to the cops. I could just be overreacting. I disconnect the call and decided to pay my pastor a visit but not before taking another peek in my review mirror. I still notice the red Bentley following but now from a distance.

I pull up to the church and Sean greets me at the front door. We go inside to discuss what happened after I picked Ashley up from the airport. I sent him a text and advised that I needed to speak with him expeditiously. I also want to make him aware of the Bentley that's been following me ever since I left home.

"You okay?" he addresses as I enter through the back of our church.

"No. I think Ashley is cheating on me with a guy named Derrick."

"I hope you have proof before you accuse her of something that may not be true."

"I don't have concrete proof but..."

"Listen," Sean interjects, "if you haven't caught that girl in the act, stop tripping. You could lose her over this. I promise you, if she's cheating, it will come out. You don't have to go searching for it."

I listen carefully to every word Sean says. I understand where he is coming from, but I'm far from stupid. The same way women have that intuition, men have them too.

"I understand, but let me tell you what happened. I went to pick her up from the airport and called her phone to let her know I was out front waiting for her. She told me she was still waiting for her bags to come while she waited at baggage claim. So being the gentleman that I am, I proceeded to tell her that I would park the car so that I could not only wait with her until her bags came down but would carry them out. Then, all of a sudden, here come her bags! She told me that she would be on her way out shortly. I'm like okay, I'll just wait here until she comes out. Five minutes pass, I get a text saying 'I'm on my way out.' I look up and see some woman sprinting at top speed in my direction. It didn't take me long to notice it was Ashley. She opened the backseat door, threw her bags inside, hoped in the front seat, and slumped down so that she couldn't be seen. I stood there waiting for a hug or kiss, and she completely disregarded me. She was running from someone or trying not to get caught, Sean. I'm not stupid."

Sean knows how much this is bothering me, but before he can respond, I continue…

"Wait, I'm not finished. We're driving home and she must've dozed off. She's talking in her sleep, saying, 'Derrick, stop baby! No, don't do that baby', and so on. I damn near crashed my car because she scared the hell out of me when she started screaming. Then to make matters worse, there's a red Bentley that's been following me ever since I left my house.

Matter of fact, they are probably out there now! They followed me to the gas station and here." I'm extremely livid. If it weren't for us being in the house of the Lord, I'd be using every profane word known to man.

Sean gets up to peek out the window.

"Oh wow, I see them. Take a look!" Sean insists.

I give Sean a dumb ass look. Clearly, I know they've been following me; why would I need to look. But I still peek out the window. Just as sure as the sun is yellow, those imbeciles are parked at the corner.

"Do you have any idea who they are?" Sean asks.

"Not one clue. All I know is that they've been following me since I left home. Now you see why I'm tripping. This isn't a coincidence. Ashley's cheating, and she's bringing that bull crap to our house."

"Do you want to handle this situation? We can go outside now!" Sean snaps.

"What if they're armed? I didn't bring my gun with me."

"Dude, this is why I always tell you to keep your gun on you. You never know what's going to happen. People are crazy as hell out here." Sean smacks his lips before proceeding,

"And besides, I have my guns in the back. You can grab the 9mm from the trunk."

Sean and I march to the back of the church where he usually parks his car. My mind is excited about what is to come, but my heart tells me to be easy. People have always told me that my heart is going to get me killed. I'm starting to believe them. I don't have the desire to confront another man and possibly shoot him. I wasn't raised to have a cold heart. Sean, on the other hand, is different. He is as excited as a kid going to Disney World. The thought of us confronting strangers while being protected by 9mm brings joy to his soul. Even though he truly is a changed man, that gangster mentality still dwells deep inside.

"Yo, maybe we should rethink this. They aren't worth us going to jail or us possibly dying."

"Man, fuck that... Sorry, Jesus," Sean begs as he looks into the Heavens, asking God for forgiveness for using that type of profanity in his house. He continues, "If we're going to do this, we need to do it now. It's clear that you've been followed. Why not take those bastards out now?"

Even though he's right, I still have a conscience and, more importantly, I'm still a man of God. Besides, I definitely don't want my best friend to go down for any of my mess.

"No. Let's put the guns up. They aren't worth it. If this situation escalates, then we can take the matter into our own hands, but for now, let's just play it by ear," I conclude.

Sean gives me a disappointed look as he stuffs

his pistol into the back of his jeans. His facial expressions soften as he pulls me in for a hug me. We pat each other on the back and agree to meet up tomorrow.

I leave the church realizing that the beautiful Bentley is nowhere in sight. I drive home to have a talk with Ashley. I rehearse repeatedly on how and what I'm going to say to her. I pray that she'll be completely transparent with me so we can possibly work through our marriage if it needs to be fixed.

As soon as I walk through the door, Ashley greets me wearing my favorite outfit—, butt naked. I'm not in the mood to make love to her, but there is no way I can tell her no. So many thoughts run through my mind; has she greeted another man the way she greets me? Did she suck on him the way she sucks on me; did she ride him the way she rides me? Those thoughts quickly fade away as she helps undress me. There are no words exchanged amongst us, just sexual moans. After I finally release everything I have inside her, we both collapse on the living room floor.

"That was amazing, baby," Ashley manages to say in between her heavy breaths.

I study her every move, from the way she kissed me to the way she felt while I was inside her. Something is different, something that I can't put my finger on at the moment. She doesn't feel the same nor does she taste the same. Even though I want to confront her about whether or not she's cheating, I decide not to. Ashley seems so excited to be in my arms, almost as if she really missed me. I don't want to ruin this beautiful moment. For that reason, I come to the conclusion to not discuss the possibility of infidelity. What's done in the dark will come to light. I'll soon find out if she's a fraud.

NINE

Ashley

I wait at the restaurant for Kia to show up. I have to update her on the latest bullshit that's been happening. Derrick has been sending me all kinds of crazy messages, asking me where I am, and why I'm not answering his calls. Then to top it all off, he followed my husband and me back to our house. As soon as Michael described the type of car that was following him, I knew it was Derrick and his little friend. I needed Kia's advice on what the hell I should do. The worse part about this is I'm still in love with Derrick and I so desperately need to see him.

"Hey, girl." Kia dryly addresses me as she kisses

me on my cheek. I knew she was going to have an attitude, which I can't understand why. It's not like she's in this mess!

"I'm going to ignore your little attitude right now and cut to the chase. I invited you here because I thought you were my girl and figured you could help me out."

"Ashley, what the hell have you gotten us into?"

"Us?"

"Yes us! If either Sean or Michael find out that I introduced you to Derrick, then it's my ass on the line too! Plus, if they find out that I've been covering for you... Oh My God! My husband will never trust me again!" Kia explains.

I am so vexed! How in the hell did she manage to make this about her! I'm the one who's in trouble. I could go to jail, lose my husband, and lose my boyfriend. I have way more on the line than this bitch!

"Are you freaking kidding me right now? Are you really making this about you? Kia, I could lose EVERYTHING, do you hear me? EVERY FUCKING THING! Yes, I've made terrible decisions, but one thing is for sure, my husband doesn't deserve any of this. How dare you make this about you! I see you're still the same selfish bitch that I met years ago. You sit up here like you're on some high horse, turning your nose up at any and everybody, pretending that your shit doesn't stink. Newsflash, boo, you must have forgotten I went with you when you thought you were pregnant by your husband and wanted to get an abortion! Oh, that's right; it wasn't by your husband but by his cousin! Since we're jogging down memory lane, let's talk about how that stripper had your legs up in the air two days before your wedding day! Yeah, bitch, don't act like I don't know your secrets! Before you throw salt, make sure you season your trifling ass with it first!"

I grab my jacket from the chair and storm out of the restaurant. I am so livid and embarrassed. How dare she not only judge me but make this situation about her. Never in my life would I ever throw anyone's past in their face, simply because my past isn't squeaky clean. However, she had it coming. Kia has always been condescending toward everyone, including me.

I reach for my keys in my purse so that I can hop in my car to drive home. I plan to figure out how to deal with all of this on my own now.

"You're right! I'm sorry!" I hear Kia's faint voice behind me.

"Come back inside please." I feel Kia's hand on my shoulder, assisting me to turn around to face her. I quickly turn around and collapse into her bosom. Kia wraps her frail arms around me and holds onto me for dear life. Kia knows how much I love her and I know she loves me; she just has some messed up ways, as we all do.

After shedding a couple tears, Kia lifts my face to wipe my cheeks. I apologize to her for the horrible things I just mentioned as she guides me into the restaurant. It's evident that I caused a scene because all eyes are on us as we re-enter the establishment.

"Table for two again please!" Kia yells.

The host cautiously walks us to the same table we were previously sitting but this time; Kia sits next to me in our booth. She grabs my hand as I lay gently on her shoulder. I embrace her caring gesture as she rests her head on top of mine. She reminds me that everything is going to be okay and that she has my back.

I catch her up on everything that transpired; from the moment I revealed to Derrick that I was married until my husband informed me that he was being followed.

"Well, how do you know it was Derrick and his friend following Michael?" Kia interjects.

"Girl, Derrick's friend, Tommy, is the only friend I know who drives a red Bentley. I just pray he doesn't hurt him. What should I do, Kia?" I cry.

We try to come up with a master plan before we're interrupted by our server. Kia and I place our orders and continue our conversation.

"Have you talked to Derrick since you ditched him at the airport?"

"No, he's texted and call, but I haven't responded to him. I want to call him so bad. I'm so in love with him, Kia. Am I wrong? Is it possible to be in love with two guys?" I flop my head down on the table, using my forearms to stop me from banging my forehead.

"Try to call him and see where his head is. Maybe if you try to talk to him, he'll change his mind."

"Girl, I hate that I have this fye coochie," I say, jokingly, and Kia laughs too. I had to break up this doleful moment.

Kia doesn't provide much advice other than me reaching out to Derrick. We eat and enjoy a couple of drinks before we part ways. We kiss each other goodbye and I watch her leave from the parking lot. As I reach for my cell phone to call Derrick, it rings. It's Derrick. My heart smiles and my face lights up like a young child on Christmas morning.

"Hey."

"Hey, Ashley."

"We need to talk. Are you home?" I ask.

"Yeah, I'm here. How long will you be?" he questions.

"Maybe fifteen minutes."

"Alright." He disconnects the call right away.

I know he is highly upset. I ran out on him at the airport a couple days ago, and I haven't returned any of his calls or texts. I'm somewhat skeptical about stopping by to see him. I'm trying to come up with a lie that can explain my unusual behavior.

As I continued down I36, headed to Derrick's, I think it will be noble to just tell him the truth. I mean, the damage is already done. Maybe I can fix it by just coming clean. Even though I am madly in love with Derrick, my husband comes first.

I pull into his driveway and run around to the side door. The rain is starting to fall heavily. I want to avoid getting my hair wet since I left my umbrella at home. Luckily, Derrick's side door awning is wide enough to keep me dry until he answers the door. I ring the doorbell twice and bang on his door so that he knows I'm not at the front. After about a minute or so, Derrick opens the door to let me in. My God, this man is absolutely gorgeous.

"Go to the basement," he directs me as I walk toward his living room since I've become accustomed to hanging out with him in there. I do as I'm told while removing my jacket. I laid my jacket across the arm of the sofa and sit toward the other end where his blanket is. I assume Derrick must've fallen asleep here since his pillows, blanket, and house slippers are present.

"I need to talk to you, baby. There's something

I need to come clean to you about." I don't look his way because I'm a coward. I don't deserve either one of these guys. Derrick doesn't respond to me and I figure it's because he already knows the truth. I turn around only to come face to face with his beautiful, nine-inch, well-crafted dagger. He wants me to suck him off. How can I say no? The idea of me revealing the truth quickly drifts away as I take all nine inches of him into my mouth. I continued pleasuring Derrick as if I'm competing for the gold medal at the Olympics.

After I finish pleasing him, Derrick takes me to his spare bedroom which is also located in his basement and makes love to me like this is his last time. He becomes redundant as he professes his love to me over and over again. As much as I want to come clean about my husband, I can't. What's a girl to do in a situation like this? I can't walk away from Derrick.

It was now seven o'clock in the morning and Derrick and I have slept the night away. I check my phone and there are over fifty text messages and ten missed calls from Michael. My throat literally falls to the pit of my stomach. What the hell am I going to tell Michael? I'm sure he has called Kia, and she had no idea that I was coming to see Derrick. She can't even lie about me staying the night with her because Sean was home. Sean would never lie for me; he is loyal to my husband.

"Is everything okay?" Derrick asks as I wake him out of his sleep with the loud rumbling I'm creating.

"No, everything is not okay, baby. I have to get home to my husband. He's going to kill me!" I don't mean it literally; nonetheless, since I created this dumb ass story, Derrick takes it literally.

Derrick doesn't say a word, but his eyes tell a different story. He's filled with rage. I run out of his house as fast as I can and hop in my car. I open my phone to read some of the messages that Michael sent me.

"Baby, is everything okay?"

"Where are you?"

"Answer the phone?"

"I just called Kia, and she said she left you over two hours ago."

"I'm calling the police!"

"Baby, please be okay. Where are you?"

I read some of Kia's messages, and they are similar to Michael's. My last resort is to call my co-worker, Ann, and ask her to lie for me. I still have a recording in my phone of her sucking her life away on a stripper the night before her wedding. I hate to be the type of female to blackmail another female, but desperate times calls for desperate measures.

"Hello," Ann manages to say through a yawn.

"Ann, it's me, Ashley. I need your help, like now. Get up."

I can hear her moving around, probably trying to

get clear of her husband. I'm certain she walks into the bathroom because as soon as she speaks her voice echoes.

"Oh my God, is everything okay?" she questions.

"Yes, well no. Everything is not okay. I hate to even ask you this, but I got into some shit last night, and I need you to vouch for me."

"What kind of trouble? And who do I need to lie to?"

"I need you to call my husband and tell him that I crashed over there last night and that I'm completely wasted. Ask him to come and get me from your house. I'm literally about five minutes away, and I can pretend that I'm still hungover." I completely avoid the question about what kind of trouble I had gotten into. I don't want this bitch to know all my business. I can't have her holding something over me that could possibly destroy my marriage.

"Um, okay, I guess. But, how am I going to do that when my husband is in the other room? He's going to eventually wake up and ask what's going on. What if he wakes up when your husband is in the house? He may tell the truth that you were never here last night."

She has a point! Thank God I'm quick on my feet.

"Well, how about we pretend that I'm about to drive home, that way we will be in my car. You can call him and pretend that you are attempting to stall me, but you don't know for how much longer. Make it dramatic; you know how you white girls do," I laugh.

"Giiirrrlllllll…" She's becoming hesitant, so I beg.

"Plllleeeaasssseeee… Ann, do this one favor for me. Please!"

"Fine, Ash, I'll do it. Where are you now?"

"I'm about five minutes away from you."

I hang up the phone with a smile on my face. I wish that bitch would've said no. I was going to send that video to her husband so quick.

In exactly five minutes, I pull up in front of her house. Ann stands outside with her pink robe and hair rollers in her hair. She hops in my car, and we greet each other with a hug. In that second, Michael calls again. I give her the phone and she takes total control.

"Hello... Oh hi, Michael, this is Ann. I work with Ashley."

There's a pause. Michael asks her something, but I can't quite make out what is being said.

"No, she's fine. I was actually about to call you. She stayed with me last night, and she's hungover. I'm actually sitting in her car in front of my house. She's trying to drive home, but I won't let her!"

I'm her silent cheerleader. I give her thumbs up while she gives me the middle finger. I try not to laugh but this girl is amazing. She could win an Oscar for her performance. She continues her conversation with Michael.

"Talk to her? Um… she may not be able to speak right now. She's slumped over the wheel."

What a fucking genius! I knew she was just as great of a liar as I am. I mouth the words, "I fucking love you," to her as she continues to fabricate this story for me.

"Okay, that's fine. It's 2135 South Watercress Avenue. Sure… you're more than welcome! See you soon!" Ann states before disconnecting the call.

"BITCH! YES!" I high-five her! I even think she is pleased with her performance.

"How far away do you guys live from me?"

"We are only about ten minutes away. He should be here anytime soon," I remind her.

She takes a deep breath in and lets me have it. "Why don't you just divorce him, girl? Why keep cheating on him? He's a good ass man! I knew that from the first time I met him years ago at the company Christmas party. I swear I love you, girl, but you make it hard for women like me."

Her callous comments have me ready to slice her throat. Did this raggedy bitch forget that she too once was a hoe? It takes me a second to get my thoughts together because not only does my mouth cut deeper than a sword, but I need her more than anything right now. My marriage is on the line, and I need her to help pull me through this.

So I opt out of giving her a piece of my mind by calling her out about her infamous blowjob on a well-known stripper the night before her wedding. Instead, I take responsibility for my behavior and agree with her.

"Ann, you are absolutely right. Michael doesn't deserve this. After this, I'm going to fix my relationship with my husband. He deserves all of me," I babble. The reality of it is I actually fear losing him. I want nothing more than to be faithful to him.

I wish I could snap my fingers and the love I have for Derrick would disappear, but it's not that simple.

Ann places her pale cold hand on top of mine. I guess that's her half-ass way of consoling me.

We wait for five minutes or so until I see headlights flying down her street. I can't make out if it's Michael or not, but we decided to get into acting mode just in case it is. I slump over the wheel, close my eyes, and pretend to be extremely intoxicated. The unidentified car is, indeed, Michael's. The tires screech as he abruptly stops the car adjacent to mine.

"Ashley!" Michael yells as he slams his car door and rushes over to me. He opens my driver side and gently lifts my head. I purposely become so weak that I slump back over my steering wheel. Ann tells Michael that I've been out here for the last hour and she had to force the car keys from my hands.

"I couldn't let her drive home like this. I am so glad that you called," I couldn't locate her cell phone last night. I see she left it in her car. Ann announces.

"Thank you so much for answering my call. I thought something happened to her. I appreciate you not letting her drive home under these conditions." Michael lifts me from my waist and drapes my limp body over his masculine shoulder. He carries me to his Mercedes and lays me in the backseat. He even brought a pillow to lay my head on. I immediately start crying because of how amazing he is. It hurts me to my core that I have resorted to all of this.

"Baby, I'm so sorry," I wail. Even though he doesn't know what I'm truly sorry for, he kisses me on my forehead and tells me that he forgives me.

Michael closes the door and goes over to Ann to grab my keys and purse, I assume. I can't quite make out what is being said as their conversation is muffled in the distance. However, I do hear Ann tell Michael to, "take care of my girl."

He replies, "I will. I'll have someone pick up her car later."

TEN

"What's up, Tommy!" I greet my guy as he enters my home. Tommy closely follows me into the kitchen.

"Are you hungry? You want a sandwich or something?" I inquire before he and I get down to business.

Tommy knows anytime I text him "9110" it's for a job. I got that code from being in the joint. 911 stands for, of course, an emergency. The number 0 is for the hole that will be left in our victim's face or chest.

"Naw, I'm good. Let's get down to business,

shall we," Tommy hints.

Tommy takes a seat at my breakfast bar as I continue to make me a ham and cheese sandwich.

"I've been thinking, how about setting this up as a robbery and killing him that way? Not in his home, too much evidence could accidentally be left behind. But when he leaves the gym after work. I already checked, there are no cameras in that parking lot, and it's pitch dark when he leaves the gym around nine pm."

"How do you know what time he leaves the gym? And what gym does he go to?"

"I have an inside connection at World Time Fitness, on Barbon Street. I told him I would give him $7000 to let me know when he comes to the gym after work."

"You trust this cat?" Tommy questions.

"Yeah! He's done a couple of jobs for me before. I told him if he comes through this time, I would permanently put him on my payroll. He's a young kid who masturbates to the idea of having money. I'm not worried about him."

"What about Ashley?"

"I'll plan another trip with her. I'll book a flight leaving out next Thursday morning to Cabo."

I must admit that what I'm doing or even thinking about doing leaves a guilty conscience on my soul. It could be that possibly I'm becoming a better man, or at least trying to be a better man. I want to leave that lifestyle behind me. I told myself years ago that I didn't want to take another man's life. The last time I actually killed a man was about six years ago. Matter of fact, he was only a kid, nineteen-years-old to be exact. I didn't want to do it, but he left me no choice. He was part of my drug operation that was destroyed by undercover cops who wired this kid up. I knew this night was different from all the rest. Even when I called the meeting a day before, my instincts told me not to. Going against my better judgment, everyone gathered at an abandoned warehouse where I moved the majority of my drug supplies. Not only was this kid late showing up, he was drenched with sweat in the heart of winter. I asked if he was okay and he nodded. I was raised in the streets, and I automatically knew when something wasn't right.

"You're sweating pretty hard, why don't you remove your coat," I remember asking him. He didn't take his coat off right away, not until I had to ask him a second time.

"Yo, what the fuck is wrong with this kid?" Tommy yelled out but not to anyone in particular.

"Grab this dude!" I requested as I watched a couple of my men snatch the frail kid and drag him toward me. I forcefully helped removed his coat and observed him tightly gripping his shirt. I pulled my gun out, placed it to the middle of his forehead, and asked him to lift his shirt. As soon as I made my request, I heard the close sounds of police sirens approaching near the warehouse. Everyone ran, but not before Tommy and two of my men grabbed the merchandise. There was an underpath that most of us took that led us two blocks away from the warehouse. Thankfully, no one was caught. Everyone was counted for the next day.

I patiently waited for Maurice—the nineteen-year-old kid—to get out of school. He was in an alternative program to receive his GED. I could see the fear in his eyes when he saw me standing on the school steps. I walked him to my car as he tried to plead his case. I kindly told him to shut up because I didn't want to make a bloody scene outside of his school. I had no problem with putting a bullet in him in front of everyone.

Long story short, I ended his life with a bullet to the head and four to his chest. I honestly didn't feel good about it. Had it not been for a couple of the guys who wanted to witness it, I would've made Maurice leave the state then lie about me ending his life.

"So you want me to fake a robbery and pop one off in him in the parking lot?"

"Yeah, you cool with that?"

"Hell yeah. I know how to stage it out. Don't worry about shit. You trying to do this next week, right? Thursday night?"

"No, wait until Friday night. I don't want it to look suspicious on Ashley's behalf. If she leaves Thursday morning and her husband is robbed and murdered that same night, the police will be all in her face. She doesn't need that type of shit right now. She's the true victim in all of this," I conclude.

"Bet, I'm down for whatever. Just make sure you get her ass out of town. I'll handle the rest," Tommy assures me.

I take out a band of $10,000 and drop it in front of him.

"You'll get the remaining $10,000 when the job is done."

Tommy puts the money inside his Jamaica Adidas jogging suit jacket and proceeds toward the door.

"Oh here, wait." I toss over a cell phone for him to use on the day he decides to rob and kill Michael. "Use this phone. Leave your cell phone at my house. Turn your auto answer on so that if anyone calls you it'll answer, and the towers will pick up your signal near my home. Also, if anyone asks, I asked you to housesit for me while I'm out of town."

"Who's the phone listed under?" he asks.

"Some Hispanic guy from Mexico! You're good, though."

Tommy walks out the door. I grab my Mac laptop and book Ashley and me a flight to Cabo San Lucas. Our flight is scheduled to leave at 7:00 am for the upcoming Thursday. I send Ashley a text message telling her that I booked our flight. She doesn't respond right away; I figure because she has some making up to do for her husband. Considering that she didn't go home last night, I know he has to be pissed. I just pray that her face wasn't the receipt of his rage.

ELEVEN

"I hope she gets what she deserves... she definitely doesn't deserve a man like Michael." I'm infuriated, explaining Ashley's actions to one of my girlfriend's from work.

Tammy actively listens to me spill the gossip about my best friend. I do love Ashley, don't get me wrong, but she was a whore; well, is a whore. She's always been that way since we were in high school. Ashley has always been self-absorbed and self-centered. Although she is a very pretty woman... actually, she is basic looking to me, but others think differently; her attitude makes her the ugliest creature on the planet. When I first introduced her and Michael at a church Christmas party, I believed he could change Ashley. I guess the saying is true, "A person won't change until they're ready to change!" Or the saying, "You can't turn a hoe into a housewife."

I knew it was love at first sight, I could see it in both of their eyes. I figured since Michael was an amazing man and he could provide Ash with something she's never gotten before, faithfulness and stability, that she would put her promiscuous ways on the back burner. Boy was I wrong! I wanted to test her, to see if she was really faithful to him and to their marriage. That's why I introduced Derrick to her. Derrick and I have been friends since college, and I knew he had many mental issues going on. Ninety percent of me knew Ashley would start sleeping with Derrick. Who wouldn't? That man is fine as hell. However, the remaining ten percent of hope I had left wishes she would have kept her and Derrick's relationship strictly professional. I should have known she wasn't shit when her husband was trying to find his fraternal twin brother, but she decided to go out of town with Derrick instead of traveling with her husband to be his support system. Instead, my husband traveled with him. Hell, even I made over fifty calls to foster homes to assist Michael in finding his brother. Ashley was too busy having a dick forced down her throat to realize how much pain her husband was in. When Michael and Sean came back from Texas, Sean told me how Michael cried when he found out that not only did he not find his brother, but his biological father was deceased. We ended up taking Michael out that evening in an attempt to keep his spirits high. He kept calling Ashley, and she never responded. I knew why she couldn't talk, but there was no way I was going to let Michael know, though. I would be breaking the girl code 101.

"Do you think I should tell Sean and let him tell Michael about Ashley?" I question Tammy.

"No, girl. Mind your damn business and let the universe expose her cheating ass," Tammy demands.

"Okay, girl, you're right. I'll just stay out of it and just pray for them. This is their issue, not mine.

Sean and I have enough shit going on to be worrying about what's going on in their marriage. He still doesn't know that we owe the IRS in back taxes." I reveal. While I agree to stay out of Ashley and Michael's problems, in my heart I know I'll carry the guilt if something fatal happens to Michael.

"Girl, how much do y'all owe? And how does he not know?" Tammy asks.

"We owe over $500,000, girl. The IRS has threatened to take our home, audit our bank accounts and everything. Even though I set up a payment plan, they are still sending threats about garnishing everything he and I own. I even hired an attorney. I honestly don't know how much longer I will able to keep this secret from him, especially if they start garnishing our wages."

"Girl, I could make suggestions all day long, but nothing is going to help with the situation you're in. That's deep!"

Just the thought of Sean finding out that I altered

our taxes every year for the last ten years just to get a large refund makes me sick to my stomach. We are so deep in debt from our maxed-out credit cards—that he still doesn't know about—to the amount I owe the IRS, that Michael Phelps would drown in it.

I cut the conversation short with Tammy because I'm starting to get a migraine thinking about the extra damage I've caused my family. When I hang up the phone, I see that I have a missed text from Ashley letting me know that she is safe and that God is still on her side. I have no idea what she's talking about, I'm just glad she's safe. Michael called us several times last night worrying about her. I texted and called her numerous times, and I didn't hear from her until a few seconds ago. I text her back, asking her what she meant by "God is still on her side." Did she almost die? Did she get hurt? I hungrily wait for her to explain what happened to her last night, which takes forever for her to do. The only reason I know she's replying because the gray bubble is visible in our text chat, indicating that she is in the process of replying. When I finally receive the detailed text, explaining how she used her co-worker to get her out of trouble because she overslept at Derrick's, I am highly disappointed. This bitch is something else. She makes me sicker by the minute.

"Who makes you sick?" my husband says. I'm so caught up in texting Ashley that I didn't hear my husband enter into the living room. Nor did I realize that I was talking to myself out loud.

"Oh, no one important, honey. One of the nurses called off again, and they want me to cover her shift tonight. I'm not in the mood to do a double so I declined," I lie.

As I listened to Sean express his deepest concerns in regards to why I need to find another job, my mind drifts to Derrick and Ashley. Why? I have no idea. I always wondered how good his sex was. Are his oral skills as immaculate as Ashley proclaims it to be? Is he really the best lover she's ever had? She's had plenty lovers so for her to give him the number one title speaks volumes.

"Baby, you okay?" Sean interrupts.

"Yes, sorry. I'm listening. I'm just a little tired this morning. I didn't get much sleep thinking about Ash."

"I know, right. I'm glad she's okay. I just hope she's not on any bullshit."

I can't understand for the life of me as to why Sean is so invested in their marriage. If he were that concerned with our marriage, maybe we wouldn't be in this predicament now. Sean cheated on me numerous times in the beginning of our marriage and without an ounce of remorse. I know he's faithful now, so that's all that matters.

"She's not. I know my girl. She's stressed. Can you imagine working as a social worker, a therapist, and still managing to obtain a 4.0 GPA while in a Doctorate program? That's enough to drive the President of the United States insane," I conclude.

"Yeah, I guess. Michael and I aren't stupid. I know you are covering for your girl, and that's cool.

I just better not find out you out here being a hoe too," he growls.

I keep my comments to myself in order to avoid a huge fight. I could easily throw his years of infidelity in his face. I have no idea what has gotten into him lately. I'm not the one who's cheating or the one who doesn't come home.

I go into the kitchen to make Sean and I some breakfast. He requested French toast so that's what he's getting. I'm not in the mood for anything heavy, so I make me a couple boiled eggs and wheat toast. We eat in silence while our thoughts blare. Deep down, I knew Sean knew Ashley was cheating. It didn't matter how much I covered for her, I knew he didn't believe me either. I decide to break the silence and ask him what is on his mind.

"Nothing at all. I'm just waiting for you to tell me the truth. You've been hiding shit from me which makes me wonder what else you're hiding."

Now I'm confused. Is he still talking about

Ashley? Or did he eavesdrop on my conversation earlier with Tammy? Regardless, I'm going to stand my ground. I'm not admitting to anything until it's proven.

"Babe, what are you talking about now?" I plead.

"Oh, so now you don't know what I'm talking about? What has gotten into you, Kia? You used to tell me everything. Now you're keeping secrets from me!"

Oh crap! He knows about our debt. I knew it was a matter of time before he would find out. I silently question myself on how long he's known about everything.

"Babe, before you start, let me explain… See, a couple of years ago…"

"No! There's no need to explain anything. You should've told me you gotten a raise at work!" Sean interrupts. He continued…"You knew damn well how much I wanted to get the basement remodeled, baby. Why would you hide this from me?" he shouts as he flashes a check stub that I kept hidden in my underwear drawer.

I didn't tell Sean about my raise simply because I knew about the debt I had with the IRS. I use the extra money to pay them back. Had I mentioned my raise, Sean would've wanted to use the extra money to build his dream basement. I want nothing more than to give him his "male sanctuary" but I think keeping our home supersedes having the basement completed.

"Babe, I wasn't trying to hide it from you. I was going to tell you about my raise soon. I was going to pay to have the basement completed for you. First, I wanted to pay off some of my credit card debts, that's all."

"You said debts as in plural, meaning more than one credit card, right? I didn't even know you had any credit cards besides the one we have together."

"These are old cards that I had in college. They

are still on my credit report, so I want to clear those up. I promise I will get this beautiful basement built just for you." I try to butter him up by walking near him and wrapping my arms around his firm body. I grab the back of his head and lean in for a kiss. We kiss and he reminds me of how much he loves me. It breaks my heart to keep this secret from him, but what he doesn't know won't hurt him. I'll figure this shit out— some way, somehow.

After Sean and I eat breakfast, we decide to catch a matinee. Before we walk out the door, I receive a message from Ash:

"Hey, girl. I'm going out of town next Thursday with Derrick. I'll be back Sunday night. Don't judge me, bitch. If the hubby asks, I'm in Houston, TX working at the hospital. That's the story, now stick to it."

I don't respond; I delete the message. I vow from this moment that I will no longer be part of her scandalous affairs. If that bitch falls, she's falling on her own. I pray that I have a front seat view.

TWELVE

NEXT THURSDAY MORNING

"I hate that you're going out of town again. You just got home," Michael whines as I pack the last of my items.

"Honey, you know my job is demanding. I hate that I'm traveling and being away from you, but when the money calls, I have to go."

"Well, are you going to go MIA like you have on all of your trips," he asks as he hands me my travel toothbrush and soap.

"No, love. I'll be in Houston so I should have service." I grab my bags and kiss Michael on the lips.

I tell him I love him before I proceed downstairs.

"Do you need me to take you to the airport or something?"

I remind him that I've already called an Uber. Moreover, I know that he has to be at work in a couple hours.

"Get some rest before you head to work. I'll call you when I'm about to board."

"Alright, call me as soon as you can. Then call me when you get settled in the hotel." He grabs one of my bags and places it over his shoulder as I open the front door. I almost grab his gym bag by accident since we have matching duffle bags. He always leaves his dirty bag near the door. That is how I know he's going to the gym after work. I would've been livid had I taken his bag by mistake. Then he would've known that this trip wasn't a business trip. I have all my sexy lingerie, sex toys, lotions and edibles in that bag.

He follows behind me as I approach my Uber

driver. We exchange kisses after he places my two bags in the backseat. Michael walks inside our home before my driver takes off. I place a call to Derrick to see where he is. He answers and says he just pulled up to the airport. I told him I was about fifteen minutes away and I would be there as soon as possible.

I know what I'm doing is wrong, but I just can't tell Derrick no. I also know what you are all thinking: *"How could she still mess with this man after he told her that he wanted to get rid of her husband."* I know, I know. I've known Derrick for years now, and I know what he's capable of. If he wanted my husband dead, he would've killed him already. Derrick is a changed man; trust me, I know. I've been counseling him and sleeping with him for over three years. He isn't going to do anything to hurt Michael.

I pull up in front of the airport, and Derrick stands there waiting for me. I notice he only has one bag, which is unusual. Derrick packs everything, even if it is a two-day trip. We greet each other with a long hug and a soft kiss on my forehead. Being the gentleman that he is, he takes my bags from my hand so I only have my purse to carry. We check our bags in and head toward the gate. Derrick texts someone as we walk, which is unusual because when we're together, cell phones are off limits.

"Who do you keep texting?" It isn't really a question but more so a statement.

"And where are the rest of your bags? You only brought one?"

"Damn, baby, you know I'm trying push this weight so that I can get rid of it. Be easy. And, yes, I only brought one bag!" he sneers, clearly becoming agitated.

"Be easy? Oh, now I need to be easy? But when I'm on my phone, I have to put it away or you're jumping down my damn throat."

He doesn't say anything, he just smacks his lips. However, he puts his cell phone away. This is just another small confirmation for me to know that I have him wrapped around my perfectly manicured finger. I could get this man to do anything I tell him to. Honestly, that's the sole reason I decided to take this trip with him. Other than the amazing sex that we have, I want to convince him to not bring any harm to my husband. My plans are to come forward and tell my husband everything and break it off with Derrick. Hopefully, everything will go accordingly.

THIRTEEN

"I'm at the airport! Let me know when you finish the work in the basement. I can't wait to see the finale." I send the coded text to Tommy. He simply replies that he will start the job later this evening. We already know what each other is referring to. I wanted Ash's husband dead! There's no way my girl will continue to be married to a man who puts his hands on her. No wonder she didn't want to come clean about her situation; she knows I have zero tolerance for that type of bullshit.

After a brief argument with Ashley about me texting on my phone, I check our bags in and receive our boarding passes. This is going to be a great trip!

I'm going to handle my business here and my boy is handling business back home.

The plane ride is a bumpy one. We run into extreme turbulence for the first thirty minutes into the flight, so there isn't much conversation between Ashley and I until the ride calms. I think we are both nervous as hell, at least I know I am. I'm not ready to meet my maker.

"Are you cool?" I manage to ask, scared shitless. I don't care how tough I may appear to be, when I'm in that moment of despair—thinking or wondering if I am going to die—I become a little girl.

"Yeah, I'm okay. I hate turbulence. Now I feel like I have to vomit. I'm so nauseous."

I can tell she is becoming ill. Her face is pale and sweaty. Her hands are clammy, and she looks as if she may pass out any minute. I signal for a flight attendant who quickly comes to our assistance. Without me saying a word and looking at Ashley, the attendant quickly reaches for a bag just in time. There is no warning. Ashley fills that large, sturdy paper bag with everything she's eaten in the last forty-eight hours. After she finishes, the attendant dumps the bag and gives Ashley a bottle of water. Ashley slumps in my lap, and I rub her back to calm her. She sleeps for the remainder of the flight.

Finally, the plane lands on the runway. I didn't think this flight would ever end. My love still isn't feeling well. Luckily, our flight attendant is extremely attentive and caring, and offers her a wheelchair and assistance to our rental. That takes a huge burden off me because I didn't know how I was going to manage to carry all of our bags and Ashley. However, I would've definitely tried to do it all. I love that girl and will do anything to bring her some comfort.

We make it to our resort right before sunset. I get Ashley settled in first, then I go back to the lobby where I ask an attendant to watch over our bags. After grabbing our luggage, I turn my phone on and wait until I'm connected to Wi-Fi. Instantly, I receive four messages from Tommy with the last one stating, "I'm on my way to do the job. Hit you when I'm done!" I grimace at the evil things that are about to occur within the next hour. I know I should not be excited about taking another man's life, but he deserves it. Right?

I ponder on that thought on the way to my room. Maybe I shouldn't be doing this, is all that I can think of. I reach for my cell to text Tommy to hold off on the job, but am interrupted by a tourist who informed me that I dropped my wallet. My mind was so consumed with the evil thought of what could've been transpiring back home that I didn't notice that my wallet was missing.

By the time I get back to the room, Ashley is snoring louder than a 600lb man. I order something light for her, a fruit tray, and I order me a double bacon cheeseburger and fries through room service. I expect us not to go anywhere tonight, considering how sick she is so I get comfortable in our master suite and wait for room service to deliver our food.

I doze off before I hear a knock at my door. Thankfully, it's room service. My stomach is rumbling louder than Ashley's snoring, which by the way hasn't eased up yet. I tip our waiter and order a show from the vast array of movies that is listed. I place her fruit inside the fridge and quickly indulge my burger and fries. I'm in the middle of watching, "She's Gotta Have It" when I receive a, "It's done!" text from Tommy.

"Oh shit!" I shout. I forgot to tell Tommy not to go through with it, at least not today. But it's too late; the job is already done. I expect Ashley's phone to be ringing off the hook all night, leading up until tomorrow morning. I'm very much in preparation to leave the following day, hence the reason I only packed one bag. Since the job has been completed, there's nothing else I can do about it other than pay Tommy the remainder of the fee and be a shoulder to cry on for Ashley.

FOURTEEN

"Did all the orders come in yet?" I yell across the room to one of my associates. I'm expecting a huge delivering of cement goods and other materials coming in today. I want to make sure I'm in the office to not only accept but to make sure every order is what I expect.

"Not yet! I just checked the tracking status, and it shows that it should be here by 4 pm!"

It isn't even near 4 pm and my work for the day is slow. I'm contemplating whether or not if I should go home and have my associate take care of the orders or just stick around and handle it myself. After thirty minutes of deliberating, I decide to stay only because I want to go to the gym tonight. I enjoy the boxing class, which I usually incorporate it into my weight training. I order the team some lunch and start working on the projects for next month. I figure there is nothing to lose if I work ahead. I try to reach Ashley and, of course, I don't get an answer. Her going out of town and not being reachable is starting to bother me. So I decide to do my own investigation. Before she left, she advised that she was going back to Texas to visit a hospital. She got the call that she needed to travel seventy-two hours prior to informing me. Ashley and I have joint Uber account so I search my email and track the receipt I received after she was dropped off. Since Uber doesn't have a customer service support number, I send an email in hopes to get some information from the driver. I make up a lie saying Ashley never made it to Texas and inquire about the time she was dropped off at the airport. I give customer service all the information about the driver and the time Ashley was picked up from our address. I make certain to ensure them that I'm just merely a concerned husband.

Once the pizza is delivered to the office and everyone partakes, I hear a notification buzz on my computer, indicating that I have new emails. I grab my plate and soda and go to my desk. I search through my emails to find the important ones first. I see an email response from Uber.

Good Afternoon,

Thank you for your email, and we appreciate your concern. We were able to contact your wife's driver, and he informed us that she was dropped off in front of the airport. He also informed us that there was a gentleman there waiting for her. There was no other information given to us. I hope this helps some.

Sincerely,

Uber Customer Support

This does not help much. I was definitely hoping for more information. However, I knew they couldn't provide more in-depth without some type of investigation report or order from the police. I decide to give this a rest. If it's meant for me to find out she's cheating, I will. Meanwhile, I can't help but wonder who this gentleman was that was awaiting my wife's arrival.

It's now approaching six pm, and my boxing class starts in forty-five minutes. Majority of my staff are already gone for the day with the exception of my janitorial staff. I shut my computer down and grab my belongings. I tell everyone good night and ride to the gym in silence. As much as I keep telling myself to stop worrying about what the hell Ashley is doing, I can't. The same way women have gut intuition is the same way I have been feeling for the last three years. That's when her behavior changed and mostly, that's when her body changed. The constant urinary infections, yeast infections, and even her bodily juices were different. I know for a fact I'm not going out of my mind. She is having an affair!

I pull into the parking lot five minutes before my workout class starts. I quickly run into the men's locker room to change so that I can get a spot first in class. As I'm leaving the locker room, I'm knocked to my feet by a man who is at least six-feet-four and has a frame stronger than Sylvester Stallone has in Rocky. Clearly, it's an accident as he reaches for my hand to help me up.

"Please excuse me. I didn't see you," the gentleman sincerely expresses to me.

"Oh, no worries, it happens to the best of us," I explain as I dust my shorts and shirt down. He began to explains that he is new to the gym and he wants to try out the boxing class.

"Oh yeah? I'm headed there now. I'll wait for you, we can go in together," I suggest. I can tell he's eager to try out the class; it's known to be one of the best cardio classes around.

"I'm Tommy, by the way," he reiterates as he reaches for my hand.

"Michael, it's nice to meet you! Now hurry up and great dressed. I'll wait for you here." I exchange the gesture by shaking his tight but firm grip.

It doesn't take long before he and I are drenched in our salty sweat. We spar with our trainer, give the punching bags our best one-two combos and do over 500 ab repetitions. By the time class is over, I have very little energy to do anything.

"You want to grab a drink when we leave, my treat?' Tommy offers. Even though I appreciate his offer, I'm too exhausted to hang out. Plus, I have to be back at work at 4:00 am because I received a new client right before I left work earlier.

"Naw, not tonight. I think I will pass. It's late, and I have to get up early in the morning for work. What about this weekend?"

"This weekend won't work for me. I will be busy. Maybe another time?" he says in his heavy Jamaican accent.

"Yeah, sure! Hopefully sooner than later," I lie. I have zero interest in hanging out with this guy. He's cool and all, but there is something eerie about him something that I just can't put my finger on. I thank

God for the gift of discernment because my radar was beeping the moment we bumped into each other.

Tommy swiftly vanishes out of the locker room. I take a quick shower, something I normally don't do but feel the need to because my clothes are completely saturated with my perspiration. I get dressed, stop by the protein bar, and order a drink. On my way to my vehicle, I pull out my cell phone to see if Ashley has called. Since there are no missed calls, I decide to give her a ring. I am so hell-bent on why she isn't answering the phone that I don't notice that I'm being followed. I call Sean to see what he's up to, but my phone is knocked from my hand as I'm tackled to the ground. I fight my attacker the best I can with what little energy I have stored inside of me. I am hit with such force that my knees buckle, and I fall to the ground a second time. I have the attacker's face mask in my hand as I take a quick glimpse of the man who is trying to murder me. I must have grabbed it from when he and I were wrestling. I'm in complete shock when I look into the eyes of the enemy because we just spent an hour working out together. Questions wander through my mind; *why would he want to kill me? What have I done to him?* I'm not sure what happens after that moment, maybe I've blacked out, but the last thing I remember is staring at the barrel of his gun. I don't know if the trigger is pulled; if I'm rescued, or even if I'm dreaming. I just remember a gun being pointed in my face and everything going completely black.

FIFTEEN

I dart out of the gym to change my clothes in the car. I parked my car approximately twenty feet away from Michael's. I put the clip in my gun, put my mask on and wait for him to leave the gym. I tried to hold small talk with him so that the individuals who were in the class would be long gone before Michael and I left. I need very little to no witnesses.

I survey the parking lot similar to the way a predator searches for their prey. Once Michael is spotted all alone, I get out of the car after scanning my surroundings. He is so distracted that he doesn't even notice me walking behind him. I know this is the moment I need to attack. The parking lot is dim, no one is around, and Michael is helpless.

I quickly run toward him, knocking him completely to the ground. Even though I thought this would be an easy victory, I didn't imagine the fight he put up. He has more skills than I expected. I am an excellent fighter, or at least I thought. I am able to get him into a chokehold, my grip cutting off his airways and causing his body to go limp. I make the mistake of loosening my grip because he's able to grab my skull mask and rips it from my face. I throw him to the ground and stand over him as I pull out my Beretta. Michael and I lock eyes for a quick second right before I pull the trigger. I leave him lying in a pool of blood as I jet to my car. I drive away as calmly but swiftly as possible.

"It's done!" I text to Derrick, reaffirming him that he no longer has to worry about this bastard. I stop near an open vacant lot. Removing every article of fabric from my body, including my gloves and mask that I took back from Michael after I shot him. I grab the lighter fluid from my trunk and douse it over the clothes. I take the lighter from the console and set everything on fire. The fire doesn't last long, but it does the job. Once the fire is completely out, I pick up the remaining remnants and throw them into the river bay. I quickly dress in the change of clothes from my backseat. I drive to Derrick's house, send him another text while sitting on his couch, and patiently wait for his approval on a job well done.

SIXTEEN

Ashley

The beaming sun wakes me up earlier than I expected. It's only 6:00 am, and I still feel the side effects of yesterday's sickness. I roll over to see Derrick sound asleep. I gently brush my hand across his smooth face in hopes to wake him up, but it doesn't work. He remains sleep, and I decide not to bother him.

I roll over to grab my phone from my purse. I have over fifty missed calls from known numbers—Kia and Sean. I only have two missed calls from Michael. I've had numerous deaths in my family to know that when someone calls you this many times something is wrong. I dread calling anyone back because I fear the worse. At least I know that my husband and best friend are okay. I decide against checking my voicemail and text messages until later.

I get up to go to the bathroom to get cleaned up. I can still taste the residue from my vomit. I brush my teeth and wash my face but there is something still sitting in the pit of my stomach. I walk outside the bathroom and look at my phone just as the screen lights up with 'Kia calling'. My intuition kicks in again, I knew something serious was wrong. Taking a deep inhale of air, I brace myself for what's to come and answer the call.

"Ashley, are you there?" she says in between sobs.

"Yeah, I'm here. What's wrong?" I mumble.

"Are you sitting down? I have to tell you something." That's it, she just confirmed what I dreaded. Something terrible has happened.

"Just tell me. What's wrong?" My voice escalates, waking Derrick out of his deep trance.

"It's… it's… Michael. He was robbed and shot last night leaving the gym. I'm so sorry, Ash. You have to come home."

My eyes grow round, and I swear my heart falls from my chest. I can barely stand as I cry out. I slide down the wall and onto the floor in a fetal position. I plead with God, asking him why he would allow something to happen to a man like Michael. Kia sobs as my cries grew louder. I know she loved Michael just as much I did. Derrick grabs my phone to talk to Kia, but my weeping drowns out their conversation.

"Come on, baby, get up. He's not dead; he's at the hospital in ICU. We have to get you home." Derrick scoops me up like a four-year-old and places me on the bed. He grabs my shoes and places them on my feet. He tries to console me but it doesn't work, only makes matters worse. Even though I'm grateful that my husband isn't dead, I want to be right where he is at this very moment. It's awkward having my boyfriend to console me as I weep over my husband. Derrick remains strong, even though I know this is hard for him.

We call a cab and head straight to the airport. Derrick pays for our tickets and gets us on the next flight back home. The stares from everyone at the airport haunts me as we wait patiently for our next flight. I want to snap at everyone who looks at me. These fools act as if they've never seen anyone grieving.

Finally boarded, the flight attendants are very sympathetic to me. They offer me water, tons of tissue, and anything else you could think of to comfort me. They check on me several times during the duration of my flight. Once we land, I quickly run out of the airport to find the Uber that I scheduled, parting ways with Derrick as he planned to wait for our bags at baggage claim. Grabbing my bags are the last of my concerns. I know Derrick will make sure my valuables are secured.

I finally pull up to the hospital where I bum-rush the check-in counter.

"Michael Thomas… what room is he in?" I'm so out of breath from running full speed from the Uber.

"May I ask your relationship with the patient?" the overweight clerk replies.

"Bitch, I'm his wife! Now, where is he?" My voice is so loud that it gets the attention of everyone around me and startles the clerk.

"He's in the ICU ward, room 1332. Take the east elevators down the hall and take it to the 13th floor. Please present them with your I.D. because they will ask for it," she calmly states.

I know my reaction was harsh, but I'm not in the mood for a Q and A session; however, I still have a heart and apologize as she remains professional during my hostility. She thanks me, and I quickly disappear from her view to go see my husband.

My heart beats faster than Gwen Torrance running in the 100-meter finals. I don't know what to expect and am petrified of what I'm about to see. I pause and take in a deep breath as I lay my head against his door and say a small prayer to God to let my husband be okay. I slowly open the door to his hospital room and walk in. I can't believe what lay before me! Michael is hooked up to at least twenty-five tubes and wires. There is blood everywhere. His face is completely bruised and severely swollen. I cover my mouth, trying to shield my cries. My husband is completely helpless, the machines doing everything for him.

I step closer and grab his hand. I lay my head across his chest and begin to pray. I pray like I've never prayed before, that's all I know to do. I need God to save my husband and bring him back to me. I pray for complete restoration, not only in his body but also in our marriage. My prayers are so intense that I don't hear the doctor enter into the room.

"I'm sorry, ma'am, I didn't want to interrupt you," the doctor deeply expresses as he checks Michael's vitals. I appreciate that he waited while I finished praying to not disturb me.

"It's okay. I'm Ashley, his wife." I extend my

sweaty hand to shake his.

"Nice to meet you. I'm Dr. Whitmore. I'll be on duty for the next eight hours."

"How is he? Will he pull through?" That's probably one of the hardest questions that I've ever asked. I'm hoping for good, though.

"I'm going to be completely honest, there may be a possibility that your husband will not pull through. There is severe damage to his occipital lobe, which not only caused the swelling on his brain but caused him to fall into a coma. The gunshot to his chest caused damaged to his lungs. We were able to go in and repair and remove the bullet that punctured his lung. We were also able to remove the bullet that struck his left testicle. During the surgery, he went into cardiac arrest. My team and I were able to revive him. We don't know how long he will be in a coma or if he will ever wake up from it. If his heart stops again, there's a strong possibility that we will not be successful in saving him. Right now, it's a waiting game. You have the option of signing a DO NOT

RESUSCITATE form; it's totally up to you. I really want you to understand the severity of us trying to resuscitate if his heart stops again; it may cause vegetative state," he sympathizes.

I stop listening after the doctor says, "vegetative state". He continues telling me everything that is wrong or could go wrong with Michael, but I don't care. I know how powerful my God is and I know he has the final say. I nicely ask the doctor to be quiet and to leave the room. He doesn't hesitate and closes the door behind him. I kiss Michael's hand and continue praying. I'm not worried about his condition because I'm confident that my husband is going to come home soon.

TWO MONTHS LATER....

There have been more than 300 visitors to see Michael during the course of his stay. I've had to put on a poker face, pretending to be hopeful. The truth of the matter is, I've lost hope that Michael may pull through. Day after day, night after night, I watch my husband, still as a board, lay in that hospital bed. The only slight improvement from the day he was first admitted is that he's now breathing sixty-five percent on his own, opposed to only forty percent. That's enough to celebrate, right? Then why do I feel like giving up and asking them to just pull the plug?

"Hi, can we talk for a minute?" A middle-aged woman asks as she enters the room. I ask Kia, who is sitting by my side, if she can hold Michael's hand until I get back. The only time I let his hand go is to use the bathroom. I haven't been home or to work. My manager was in a similar situation a year ago, so she understands what I'm going through. Unfortunately, she had to bury her husband.

We walk to the small conference room right outside the ICU. She offers me a bottled water which I happily accept.

"Let me introduce myself. My name is LeeAnn Waters, I'm the billing clerk and I just want to go over a possible payment plan for your husband. We haven't been able to get in touch with his insurance company after we sent the bill to them. Are you sure he is medically insured?"

"Of course, he is. He owns his construction company, and he mandated medical insurance to his employees so why wouldn't he have insurance?" I question.

"Okay, we will keep trying. Unfortunately, we do need some sort of payment so we need to set up a plan."

"How much do you need right now and how much is his total bill?" I inquire.

The clerk turns to the last page of his chart. Before speaking, she glances over the document.

"Well, this wouldn't be the final bill but as of right now, a payment of $6200 would cover the last two months that he's been in here."

"Sixty-two what? You mean to tell me, I have to pay almost $3100 a month for him to just lay in that damn bed? Are you fucking crazy?" I hurl.

"That's only until his insurance is cleared. Look,

I know this is hard for you; trust me, I know. The last thing I want to do is ask for money when anyone is dealing with this type of pain, but it's company protocol. We have to secure a payment soon," the clerk sympathizes.

I'm so overwhelmed. It's not that we don't have the extra money to cover his hospital bills' it's just that I don't want to tap into our savings when I know for sure he is medically insured. There is no way that I'm going to ask our friends for any money. Kia and Sean are going through their own issues. However, I know one person who would definitely help me out and even though I've neglected him and his calls the last couple of months, I know he loves me and will help me in any way he can.

"I'll get it to you by the end of this week. Will that be okay?"

"Yes. I'll touch base with you then," the clerk concludes.

As I exit the small conference room, I reach for

my cell and dial Derrick's number. He answers on the first ring.

"Hey, baby. How's your husband doing?"

"He's doing better, but not as good as I hoped. I don't mean to bother you, but I need a huge favor."

"Whatever you need, just let me know," he eagerly announces.

"I need to borrow $6500. The hospital is asking for it because they haven't been able to get in contact with my husband's..."

"You don't need to explain. I'll send it to your account shortly," he cuts me off. I know that this is difficult for him, but I had no idea that he would willingly help me out.

"Derrick, I do love you and I really do miss you. I just need to handle this situation right now. I hope you can understand," I murmur.

"Just take care of what you need to do. Text me to let me know when the money is in your account," he says as he disconnects the call. This is the first time that Derrick never told me he loves me too. I know he's upset, I could hear it in his voice, but I have no other choice. I'll just have to worry about Derrick later. Right now, my primary focus is my husband, and I'll cross that bridge with Derrick when the time comes.

SEVENTEEN

"Can you believe this bitch! She just had the audacity to ask me for money for her punk ass husband! I can't believe you didn't make sure that motherfucker was dead! What the hell do I pay you for?" I hiss at Tommy, who sits directly across from me in my living room, looking like a deer caught in headlights.

"I shot him twice in the chest and somewhere else. How did he not die?"

"You tell me! You were there! You should've made sure he wasn't breathing by sending the next bullet through his skull. I gave you one job and one job only, and you failed me!"

Tommy doesn't say much; I mean, he doesn't have much to say. He has to return the money that I gave him for this job. He sits there with a smug look on his face while I continued to drill into him. I remind him how lucky he is that he's my best friend; otherwise I would've had to kill him.

"Have you ever thought of the possibility that she could be lying about their marriage?" Tommy finally speaks after a couple minutes of silence.

"What the hell are you talking about?"

"I'm just saying, think about it! If he was beating her ass the way she claims he was, why is she going so hard for him when she has a guy like you. Something just doesn't seem right about this whole situation. I know you love this girl, but analyze this whole situation."

Tommy's making a lot of sense, even though I want to jump across the room and knock him the hell out. Quiet as I've kept, I've considered the same thing. That's why I got so upset with Ashley after we spoke earlier. She hasn't returned my calls or texts but has the nerve to ask me to pay for her husband's hospital stay. The whole time she was talking to me, I wondered why she was right by his side and not by mine.

"Don't worry about all of that. I'll get to the bottom of it. Meanwhile, I'm about to send her the money she's asking for."

"I just want you to be careful with her, I don't trust her."

"Oh, don't worry, I will!"

EIGHTEEN

"You want anything to eat?" I ask Ashley as I leave Michael's room to make my way to the cafeteria located on the first floor of the hospital. I haven't left Ashley's side unless it was to go to work. Any day I have off, I spend it with her and Michael.

"Just a bag of chips. I'm not really hungry," she utters with much fatigue.

I run down to the café to grab her some chips and me a cheeseburger with fries. I want to discuss the idea of Derrick having something to do with Michael's attempted murder. I'm assuming Ashley hasn't thought of that possibility because she's been so caught up with Michael. We all know what

Derrick is capable of, and he made it very clear to Ashley that he would hurt Michael. I've battled myself back and forth on how to approach this conversation with Ashley. I think now is the time.

"Here are your chips. I didn't know what kind to get you, but you can't go wrong with cheese Doritos." I hand her the king-size bag and sit my meal down on the mini table adjacent to Michael's bed. The repetitive beeping sounds of all his machines are driving me insane. I look at him laying helpless and say another quick prayer for him.

"These are fine, thank you," Ashley says as she scarfs the chips down her throat. She seems in a better mood from earlier today which is a good sign.

"What did that lady want to talk to you about in the conference room?

"Oh, you know, trying to get almost $6,200 out of me because they can't verify his insurance."

"He does have insurance, right?" I inquire.

"Of course, he does… I mean, I hope he does. I assume he does."

"Ashley, do you need some money? I can help you out, and you can pay me back whenever." I blurt out. She seems oblivious to whether or not he is insured. I have extra money saved so I can help her out.

"Girl, no. Don't worry about me! Besides, I reached out to Derrick and he just sent me $6500 about five minutes ago."

"You actually asked Derrick, your boyfriend, to send you some money for your husband? Girl, can I borrow your vagina powers please?" We both break out into laughter. I'm dead serious. What kind of vagina does she have between her legs? I need that kind because I couldn't ever find a man to pay for anything for my husband.

"No, but on a serious note…" I begin with sincerity. "Have you ever wondered that perhaps Derrick had something to do with what happened to

Michael?"

Ashley doesn't say anything but responds with a blank stare. I've always wondered if she considered the thought of Derrick hurting Michael.

"Do you really think Derrick had something to do with this?" she whispers.

"Um, duh! Yeah! Think about it, Ash. He told you out of his mouth that he was going to hurt Michael, and I told you that he would! He's not a man that reneges on his word. If he said he was going to do it, then he's going to do it," I reiterate.

A tear falls from her eyes. I'm not trying to hurt her, but I want to bring awareness to the type of man Derrick really is. Don't get me wrong, he's a great guy but he has another side of him that only a few people know about.

"I'm sorry, but if Derrick had anything to do with this, you need to cut him off and go to the police," I respond while wrapping my arm around her shoulders.

She snatches her frail body from my arms and walks over to where Michael lay. She grabs the chair and pulls it closer to him. She sits and weeps over his almost lifeless body. My heart breaks into a million pieces, but not for Ashley—for Michael. If it wasn't for her infidelity then we probably wouldn't be sitting here in the ICU.

"Derrick wouldn't do this. I know him. He wouldn't harm a fly. He's all bark but no bite. Let's change the subject before he wakes up and hear us," Ashley mumbles.

I don't say anything else. She talks to Michael as I continue to eat my burger and fries. I know this would be a touchy subject, but my job here is done. I put the bug in her ear, and I hope she takes in what I said... I hope. I will talk to Derrick about this when I get an opportunity but for now, I will be here for my friend the best I can.

NINETEEN

God,

I know you to be a healer. You said in your word, 'by your stripes we are healed.' I don't ask for much, but I'm humbly asking you to heal my friend. Send your healing angels to camp around his bed. Touch the hands of the nurses and the doctors that handle him daily. I pray for complete restoration and complete healing in his body. This accident was no fault of his own. I demand no permanent injuries or scars. We thank you in advance for his healing. We praise you for what you are about to do. We are about to witness a miracle! I'm going to continue to stand on your word and believe that my brother is healed. We will continue to give you the Glory.

In Jesus name, Amen

I sit back and wonder who in the hell would do this to him. I should've gone to the gym with him that night then none of this would've happened. I can't believe someone tried to kill him. It's been months and the most progress we've seen is his breathing. I mean, I'm grateful for whatever, but Michael doesn't deserve this. I know this has something to do with Ashley and whoever followed Michael to the church that day.

I can't stand the sight of Ashley. Every time she enters the room, it takes all of me not to choke her. I have to keep it cool for the sake of everyone. Besides, Michael would be devastated if he knew I choked his bitch up even though we both know she deserves it.

"Hey, brother, how are you holding up?" Ashley asks as she sits next to me in the waiting room. I had stepped out momentarily to give her and Michael some privacy. Kia just left about an hour ago to go to work, but I decided to stay.

"I'm okay. How are you holding up?" I hesitate. I really don't care, but I have to play the caring and compassionate role.

"I'm fine. Just waiting for him to wake up. He's going to wake up you know. I will be right beside him holding his hand. I know there's nothing too hard for our God, so I believe he's going to bring Michael out of this coma."

That's the only thing she and I have in common, we both believe that God is going to open his eyes so it's easy for me to be empathic when it comes to that. Otherwise, I didn't want to hear anything else she has to say. I excuse myself and tell her that I want to go back into the room so that I can talk to Michael right quick. She's okay with that, sits back and pulls out her cell phone. I consider eavesdropping to see who she is about to call but decide against it. It isn't a secret that everyone, including me, knows Ashley is a cheater. At first, I thought Michael was hallucinating. However, after noticing all these trips, the thirty-minute follow by some creeps, and Kia finally relaying to me that she thought she was cheating; I became a believer and lost all respect for Ashley. The only reason I haven't had a chance to tell Michael is because someone tried to kill him. I plan to inform him about this other man she's sleeping with as soon as he becomes 100 percent.

"Bro, I need you to wake up," I whisper as I sit next to Michael's bed. His body is so feeble it almost looks as if hurts for him to even breathe. I continue, "I miss you so much, bro. You're my only friend. We were supposed to go bowling a couple of weeks ago, remember? We need to reschedule so I can kick your ass out there." I chuckle but he doesn't. Michael is known to talk shit and to be extremely competitive, that's what I admire about him most.

"I need you, man. I need you here with me. I know you can hear me, I need YOU. You promised that we would grow older together. You promised that we would raise our children together. Remember you said you would name your first born after me?

Well, you need to be here to do that! You are the toughest guy I know, so I need you to fight. Keep fighting please!" I try to keep my composure, but no man wants to see anyone he loves like a brother laying lifeless in a hospital bed. Michael doesn't even look the same; he has to have lost more than thirty pounds. His muscle mass has vanished; he's nothing but skin and bones.

I stand up to start doing some exercises with Michael to keep his blood flowing by moving each leg back and forth fifteen times. I do three sets of those on both legs. I do the same thing with his arms until I'm interrupted by one of the nurses.

"Those exercises are really good for him, make sure you continue doing those," she reminded me. I don't respond but notice her turning down his breathing machine.

"Why are you turning down his air?" I question.

"Well, he's starting to make a lot of progress. We are going to see how well he can breathe on his own if we turn the machine down to thirty percent, which means he will be breathing seventy percent on his own. We just got his scan results back and everything looks normal. Honestly, I think he's going to be fine once he wakes up from this coma, but please don't quote me; I'm not a doctor. All his vitals look good; we just have to wait until he opens his eyes."

I almost break down listening to the nurse. This is definitely good news because I'm beginning to question my faith.

"Keep talking to him, he can hear you," she tells me as she exits the room as quickly as she entered.

TWENTY

Ashley

Another three months have passed and my husband is still in the hospital, but now he's no longer in a coma. He awakened about a month ago and was transported out of ICU. His breathing tube was removed, but he's still nonverbal. There was severe damage done to his vocal cords so surgery is scheduled late next week to repair it. Even though Michael can't talk, he communicates in other ways. He's regaining his strength and movement in his lower body. All his neurology and cat scans have come back completely normal. He still had months of rehab, but I'm grateful for the progress he's made.

"Call me. I need to taste you." I receive the text

from Derrick. I really don't want to leave my husband, but I'm so sexually frustrated. It's been almost a month since I last seen Derrick. I know what you are thinking; I'm trifling, right? I honestly don't care. I'm in love with both men, and I'm not going to neglect either of them.

"Where are you?" I reply.

"Home. Come see me for a few minutes."

"Okay, I'm about to leave the hospital. Give me about fifteen minutes."

"Take those panties off before you get here. I'll leave the door unlocked. Come on in. I'll be waiting in my bed for you."

I instantly get wet. Just imagining what he's about to do to me makes me so horny. I walk over to Michael and tell him I'll be back in a couple of hours because my job has called me in. Michael mouths the words, "I love you, see you later!" and I repeat back to him after I kiss him on the forehead. I leave his room and rush to the nearest bathroom. I remove my underwear and bra and place them in my purse. I freshen up a little by using some soap and water, then I hurry to my car. I call Derrick to let him know I'm in route.

I pull up to Derrick's home, and my hormones start racing. My nipples are so hard that they could honk my car horn by themselves. I walk up to his door and open it. I remove every piece of my clothing and leave them where I drop them. I walk upstairs to his bedroom to find him laying naked, exposing what God created—a masterpiece.

"I see you're waiting for me, huh? You must miss me." I seductively mention as I began to caress my breasts. He has that sexy smirk on his face; you know the smirk of self-confidence.

"Of course I miss you. Why don't you come over here and let me show you how much." He massages his manhood, but I demand him to stop so I can finish. I seductively walk toward him and grab his dick from his hands so that I can gently place it in my mouth. I work my tongue and jaws until he can barely take it.

"Don't stop, baby. Right there," he manages to say in between his soft yet masculine moans. As soon as he was about to climax, he lifts my head and makes his demands.

"Turn that ass around so I can taste you too. I want us to come at the same time." I straddle his face and insert his dick deep down my throat. It doesn't take more than ten seconds for us to orgasm, and we devour each other's juices.

He taps my ass, which indicates that he wants me to lay down on the bed. We're in sync with each other. I know what each tap, movement, and moan means. He spreads my legs so wide that I may pull a groin muscle. Thank God he's still hard enough to please me. He slides inside me while he kisses me, which makes me orgasm again. This man drives me wild. The way he pleases me is beyond what Michael has ever done. The way he makes love to my neck and to both breasts while he continues stroking me makes me orgasm a third time. I feel my dampness making a puddle under my ass, and I can tell Derrick is about to come again at any moment. I want this exotic ride to last a little longer.

"Hit it from behind, baby," I beg. He anxiously obliges. I turn around and toot my ass up high enough to give him easy access. He drills in me so hard; I have to bite down on the pillow just so I won't scream out. He finally releases weeks of his build-up inside of me; at least it better have been weeks. I would be devastated if I found out that Derrick is seeing someone else.

We collapse onto his bed and try to catch our breaths. He turns on the fan that is next to his bed so that we can feel some air. He wraps his arms around me, and I rest my sweaty head on his chest. The thought of Kia believing Derrick had something to do with the attempt on Michael's life is absurd but not impossible. I know how Derrick feels about me, and I know he would go to any length to protect me. I hate that I lied and said my husband beats me. If I could take back any moment, that would be one.

"You know, I sat with Kia a couple of weeks ago and she mentioned something to me that has been weighing heavy." I start the conversation as we intertwine our fingers with each other's. I know this conversation could possibly escalate but part of me wants to know the truth.

"Yeah? And what's that?" he questions.

"She believes that you had something to do with Michael getting shot. Of course, I didn't believe her, and I made sure I shut those speculations down quick too," I reassure.

There's an awkward moment of silence before he speaks.

"Why would she think I would do anything like that in the first place?"

"See… what had happened was…"

"Damnit, Ashley!" he yells as he gets up from his bed to put on his clothes. I've pissed him off by opening my mouth to Kia, but she's my best friend, who else am I going to vent too.

"Did you go back and tell Kia that I was going to kill him?" he snaps.

"No! Yes! Wait…" a moment of realization dawns on me, "Did you have something to do with this?" I scream.

"Are you being serious right now? No, I didn't have anything to do with your husband. If I did, trust me, you would've buried him months ago!"

A large lump forms in my throat. The idea of me burying my husband strikes a nerve. He knows he hurt my feelings which is the reason why he gets back in bed with me.

"Ashley, I'm sorry. I meant that if I had done the job, it would've been done correctly, but I didn't do this. Actually, I've been doing some thinking, and I think it's best that we part ways. You need to focus on what you got going on in your home. I can't continue to wait for you. Even though I love you, I deserve better than this," he murmurs.

201

"Derrick, I can't live without you. Please don't give up on me. I'm going to leave him, I promise I am. I'm so in love with you, I would be heartbroken if you left me right now," I lie. I have no intentions on leaving my husband, and I have no intentions on Derrick leaving me. I'm going to have them both, and if I have to keep selling them lies, by all means, I'm going to keep lying.

I leaned over to kiss Derrick, and he kisses me back. I know I have him wrapped around my finger. He isn't going anywhere, and I'm not going to let him go that easily. We make love once again, and we both doze off into the night.

THE NEXT MORNING

"Oh shit!" I say as I quickly get out the bed to head to the bathroom to wash up. I check my phone that's on the nightstand. Kia and Sean must have called over ten times each. I immediately call Kia back.

"Girl, where are you?" she inquires.

"Sorry, I got off work late and needed some rest. So I decided to go home and sleep in my bed. You know damn well that sofa in Michael's room is destroying my back." I fib.

"Well, you need to bring your ass to the hospital! Michael just said his first words, and you missed it," Kia informs.

"Really, Kia? Oh my God. What did he say?" I beam with excitement. I make sure my voice is low so that I don't startle Derrick, so I turn the shower on so that he can't hear my conversation.

"He said and I quote, 'Where's my Ash?'"

I place the phone to my heart and cry.

"I'm on my way!" I softly cry out to Kia. I disconnect the call, wiped my face down with my hands and hop in the shower. Thankfully, I have a toothbrush and extra clothing here at Derrick's house. It would look suspicious if I walked back into the hospital smelling fresh but have on the same clothes I had on the night before. I could've easily gone home, but that would've taken me twenty minutes out of my way.

I get dressed, kiss Derrick on the lips, and tell him that I'll text him later. I nearly hit eighty miles-per-hour in route to the hospital. I'm surprised I don't get pulled over. I'm so excited to see Michael and to hear his voice. I almost wish I stayed at the hospital last night. As soon as I enter into the room, I see my husband sitting upright eating on some Jell-o. My knees nearly buckle at the sight of how amazing he looks. He smiles at me, and I smile back. I rush toward him to hold him. Kia and Sean stand back to admire our sincere moment. I cry like a baby, and I thank God for turning this situation around.

"How are you feeling this morning?" I ask. He can't say much, considering he still has to have surgery on his vocal cords, but he writes on a piece of paper...

"I'm okay. My voice is still sore. How are you? You look stunning." He ends the sentence with a smiley face.

"So do you. I can't wait until you come home for good."

"Me either." He writes. A couple of doctors coming into the room disturbs our moment. They want to discuss some things with Michael and I wanted to listen, but my stomach has another agenda. I try my hardest to stay, the contents of my stomach rumble during the discussion. I excuse myself while the doctor explains the side effects of his lung being punctured and what to expect from the upcoming throat surgery. I trot to the nearest bathroom with joy in my heart. The thought of my husband being alive made me cheerful. His heath was all that matter. I sent a silent 'thank you' to the man above and made another vow to be faithful to Michael.

TWENTY-ONE

It's been almost six months since I've been in the hospital, and I still can't recall the moments that led me here. The last thing I remember is me being at work, eating pizza. I was told that I was shot leaving the gym. Although my memory is vague, I'm grateful to be alive. Part of me remembers going to the gym that evening and meeting someone, but I can't decipher between it being a repetitive action or me actually remembering that night. It wasn't uncommon for me to go to the gym or was it uncommon for me to meet new people there. I just wish I could regain some of what happened that night.

"You ready for physical therapy?" my therapist asks as she enters my room. I absolutely hate therapy, and I've only been doing it for a week now. I'm scheduled for therapy for the next twelve weeks, four times a day. I also have speech and occupational therapy, which is scheduled after the duration of my physical therapy.

"As ready as I can be," I fib. I send Ashley another text to let her know that I'm on my way to physical therapy just in case she comes into my room looking for me. I don't expect a prompt response from her; actually I've stopped expecting pretty much anything from her. I may have a bit of amnesia, but I haven't forgotten how suspicious her behaviors were and are. Nothing much has changed. She's gotten so bold to the point where she came to the hospital last week with the scent of another man's cologne on her. I didn't say anything because, well, I couldn't talk that well yet. I recently had surgery on my vocal cords.

The only thing that keeps the spark between us

is that she makes love to me after the doctors and nurses make their rounds. She has mastered the art of giving me fellatio and riding me in this weirdly shaped, uncomfortable bed. She's given me this type of loving at least once a week since I've been out of my coma. That was nice and all, but I am far from incompetent. She comes to the hospital hours after she gets off work; I mean like six to seven hours later. Some days she doesn't even come nor can I even reach her. I decide not to dwell too much on this until I become 100% healthy. If she's not open to therapy, then I may suggest that we separate until we come to a mutual agreement on how we should proceed with this marriage or divorce.

"Okay, Mr. Williams, I need you to help me out and lift yourself up. On three, ready; one...two...three..."

I do as my therapist asks and lift myself so that she can position me into the wheelchair. We ride in silence down to the first floor. The smell of death lingers throughout the halls. I can hear a family crying and another patient scream out in agony, begging for painkillers. Being in a hospital is draining, both spiritually and physically.

We finally reach the therapy room, and there are three other patients already using the equipment. I'm positioned on the stationary bike first.

"Okay, I want you to warm up for about twenty minutes," Christiana, my therapist, suggests as she transitions me from the chair onto the bike.

I'm not completely paralyzed, but I don't have much feeling in my lower body. I'm able to lift my legs and position each one into the pedals so that I can ride. Christiana sets the timer and the pace, and I begin to peddle. I instantly feel the blood flow throughout my legs and sudden fatigue. It hasn't been three minutes yet and I'm about to pass out. I completely understand that everything is a process but being an athlete to barely being able to ride a bike for three minutes without passing out is a hard pill for anyone to swallow.

I gut out the twenty minutes before Christiana comes over to relieve me. My next task is squats while using the parallel bar as a crutch. I complete four sets of twenty reps on each side easily.

"You are in a great mood today I see. The wife must have taken care of you this week." Christiana smirks and winks. I'd disclosed to her how my wife makes love to me in the room a couple times a week. She's actually the one who recommended that we have sex. She believes that will help with the blood circulation in my lower body. I'm thankful that I can feel every bit of the sexual gratification. That's probably the only area that isn't completely numb.

"That she did, but that's not the reason as to why I feel good. I'm so motivated, I just want to hurry and get out of here so that I can resume to my normal activities. Does that make sense?" I question as I continue to take step by step toward the end of the bar. I'm determined to walk without any assistance very soon. I've given myself three weeks to master the parallel bar and an additional four weeks to walk without any help. I don't care if I only take two steps, just as long as I'm walking.

"That makes total sense." She grins. "Keep grinding the way you are and you will walk out of this hospital in no time."

I keep those words embedded in my memory. I might have forgotten some of my past events, but I won't forget those words of motivation from Christiana.

Therapy lasts for another hour. We spend the rest of our session doing stretch exercises, deep tissue massage, and stem treatment. I'm beyond exhausted and ready for dinner and a nap. My therapist rolls me to my room where Ashley and Kia greet me.

"How did this handsome man of mine do today?" Ashley asks proudly.

"He's amazing! He's actually one of my best patients. He's making great progress and if he keeps this attitude up, he will be walking on his own very soon. So whatever you're doing to him, keep it up." We all laugh in unison, except for Kia. She appears to have a chip on her shoulder, but I'll soon figure out what the hell is going on with her.

Both the therapist and Ashley assist me as I climb into my bed. I see the menu for dinner beside my bed and proceed to fill it out. Ashley's phone rings and she excuses herself to take the call. She claims it's her job, but I find it extremely odd that every time she's around me, her phone is Gorilla Glued to her hand. Kia must notice my vibe and asks if I was cool.

"You cool?" Kia asks, her brow cocked.

"Yeah, why would you ask me that?" I mumble. It's evident my demeanor quickly shifted.

"Look, you know you and I have been like brother and sister to each other. You also know that I don't sugar coat shit; if I smell bullshit, it's bullshit!" she snaps.

She's right. I've known Kia just about my whole

life, and she's always been one to speak her mind. She's definitely a ride or die type of chick, and she can hold her own. Women don't really vibe well with her because she's out of their league. Kia's beautiful, and I mean drop dead beautiful. To the put the icing on the cake, she's extremely smart with a banging body. She loves working out and takes pride in the way she looks. I don't think Kia ever steps out of the house without looking like she belongs on the red carpet. Even her nursing scrubs are custom-made to hug her small frame. Every pair of shoes she owns are Red Bottoms. I never question where the money is coming from, I just assume Sean was holding out on me by telling me his annual income in a previous conversation years ago. It isn't my business, so I make sure that I don't make it my business.

"Kia, what are you trying to say?" I spit.

Right before Kia spills the beans, Ashley walks back into the room.

"Sorry, guys, had to take that call. Work, work, work!" she sings.

Neither Kia nor I say anything; we just glance at her and continue our fake conversation so that Ash doesn't take it that we were gossiping about her or, at least, about to start.

Ashley sits on the side of my bed and circles an extra order of French fries off my menu. She calls the RN so that they can put our order in. I asked for the baked fish, mashed potatoes, and string beans. Kia and I side-eye each other, indicating that we both know Ashley is full of shit. Nonetheless, I still love her and want to be with her. She is my rock, and I pray that I'm still hers.

"How was work today, best friend?" Kia asks.

"Long and tiring, but it was cool. How was your day?" Ashley hesitates, which I don't blame her. Kia's tone throws us both completely off.

"Fine! I'm about to head home. I need to get dinner started. I'll see you guys later." Kia approaches and kisses my forehead and pinches my shoulder without Ashley noticing. She hugs Ashley and tells her she'll call her tomorrow.

"What the fuck is up her sleeve?" Ashley snarls. "She's been acting weird ever since you woke up from your coma."

"I have no idea." I fib. I'm undecided if I should bring up the cheating allegations now or just wait until I'm 100 percent. I guess it doesn't matter because, of course, her phone rings again and she runs out of my room.

TWENTY-TWO

Ashley

"Babe, what's up? I'm at the hospital." I inquire. Derrick has called me back to back all day.

"What time are you leaving? I need you to hide a couple of bricks at your house. You know I'm trying to sell this house, so I need to get some of this stuff out of here," he replies.

"Derrick, you know how I feel about holding your drugs. I've asked you not to get me involved in your illegal mess. I thought you were done with that lifestyle? Have you been lying to me?" I whisper. I don't want to risk Michael hearing my conversation nor do I want to walk all the way to the end of the hallway to sit in the waiting room.

"Babe, I been done pushing dope. I'm giving the remainder to my homeboy to do whatever he wants with it. I'm about to get my real estate license in a couple of weeks. I'm trying to turn over a new leaf for me and for us."

"Alright, I'll come get it."

"When?"

"When I leave the hospital! What's up with the twenty-one questions?" I hiss.

"What time will that be?" he completely ignores my question.

"Derrick, maybe in the next hour or so. Is that okay?"

"Yeah, that's cool. Just hit me when you get outside. I'll come out and put it in your trunk. Just hide it in your garage or somewhere no one will suspect anything, please. I'll come back for it in a couple of weeks," he orders.

I feel like I'm one of his men working for him. I

understand how the game works. If I were pushing that much weight, I would have my merchandise secured in different places. But, why me? This is the second time he's asked me to hold his drugs. I guess I should be flattered. That means he trusts me. It seems as if our dynamic has suddenly changed within the last two weeks. I don't understand why or how. I make love to him almost every day and cook his meals. I try my best to make him feel secure enough to know that I'm going to leave my husband once he is better. Even though that is far from the truth, but Derrick doesn't need to know that.

"How's everything going at the hospital? What are the doctors saying?"

"Not too good, he's still in a deep coma. The doctors don't know when he will wake up from it. We are hopeful and praying that everything will be okay," I misinform. There is no way I'm going to let him know my husband is up and moving around. He'll be jumping down my throat for me to leave him.

"Damn, well keep me posted. I know you are at the hospital, I'll let you go."

Something speaks to me and tells me to just end the relationship with Derrick. Here I am, trying to please a man who claims he loves me but is willing to risk me going to jail for holding his dope. I can't shake this weird feeling, but I know I have to end this quick. I'll stick to my commitment and hold his bricks, but that's it. There will be no more Derrick and me... I think.

I sit with my husband for a couple more hours before he finally dozes off for the night. There are times I stay the night with him but every time I do, I wake up with a sore back and a stiff neck. Someone should make beds for the comfort of loved ones and visitors who choose to stay the night. I advise Michael that I'll be back first thing in the morning. I am off work and nothing will bring me joy than spending the whole day with him. I send Derrick a text letting him know that I'll be pulling up to his house in fifteen minutes. I even make it known that

I'm not coming inside and to bring his items to the car.

"I'll contact you later baby." He rushes to kiss me on the cheek after he dumps his red duffle bag inside my trunk.

"This will be the last time I hold any of your products. Once the dust settles, make sure you come and get your shit." I hiss.

He walks inside his home and quickly I remember Kia's actions earlier in the day. The way he brushed me off struck the same nerve. Actually, she's been shady toward me for the last couple days. I grab my cell phone to give her a call.

"Yeah?" she answers with an attitude.

"Really, Kia? What the hell is up with you? You've been acting funny as hell toward me. What did I do to you?" I rebut.

"Are you kidding me right now? Your husband needs you and you keep dipping off with Derrick!

We all know Derrick had something to do with Michael being in the hospital, but yet, you're still sucking his dick!"

I can't believe this bitch has the audacity to come at me over some shit that doesn't involve her ass. Subsequently, she doesn't know that I'm en route to her house to whoop her ass. I know she's home alone because Sean was entering the hospital as I was leaving.

We continue our bickering until I'm parked in front of her house.

"Kia, you talking all that tough shit now, come outside. I'm here waiting for you! I want you to say everything you just said to my face."

"My pleasure!" She disconnects the call. I'm so infuriated. I get out of the car and wait on her porch for her to come outside. What I don't know is that Kia can apparently fight. I underestimated her. I hate to admit it, but she kicks my ass. I'm punched, thrown off the porch, kicked, stomped, slapped…you name it, she does it. Even though I lose that battle, it isn't an easy victory for her either. I give it my all and she's left with a couple of bruises from my right hook, but nothing compares to the injuries I'm left with. I'm pretty certain my eye is blackened and my nose is broken, or at least that's what I think.

I'm exhausted from our brawl, and I lay helpless in her front yard. Kia, who stands with all power over me, grimaces at the torment I'm experiencing. I feel helpless and start crying. I'm over-emotional, can't really understand why. It could be that I feel embarrassed by getting my ass kicked, or knowing that this is the end of our friendship, or maybe the fact that I know what I'm doing is wrong and everything is all my fault. I have to accept the blame! I put not only Michael in this terrible situation but Derrick, Kia, and Sean. I've lied to everyone for my own personal satisfaction.

Kia squats down near me and helps me up. She drapes my arm around her shoulder while she gently places her arm around my waist to provide assistance as she guides me into her house. She sits me on her sofa and goes to her kitchen for two pieces of cold meat. She hands me a frozen steak to place over my eye and she places her frozen steak to Band-Aid her left cheek.

"What has gotten into you, Ashley? How could you not see that Derrick has something to do with this?" she sincerely expresses.

"Kia, I fucked up. This is my entire fault. I'm so sorry, I'm so sorry," I bawl. I weep so much that it brings me to my knees, giving an uneasy, nauseated feeling. Before I know it, I decorate Kia's rug with the dinner I had earlier. I can't stop myself, I continue until there is nothing left inside of me.

I feel the gentleness of Kia's hand resting on my back, asking if I'm okay. She wipes my mouth with the paper towel she retrieved from her kitchen.

"Luckily, I was throwing this rug out; otherwise, I'd have to kick your ass again." She chuckles. I don't really find it amusing that I got my ass kicked, but to lighten the mood I laugh too as she rolls the vomit-filled rug up.

"Fuck you! You're lucky I've been sick!" I joke.

"Sick? What's wrong with you?"

"I've just been extremely tired lately. I wake up with no energy; I go to bed with no energy. I woke up nauseous the other day and as soon as I got to work, I was making love to the urinal."

"Um, you're not pregnant, are you?"

"Hell no! I just got off my period last week. Plus, I take my birth control faithfully," I hiss.

"Girl, that doesn't mean a thing. I was on birth control and I had a period. Sean and I got pregnant."

"Bitch, a lie! Your ugly ass can't have kids because of the accident. Quit trying to get me upset, heifer." That makes us both laugh. Kia knows damn well she's never gotten pregnant, and she lied to use that scare tactic against me. I can't stand her ass, but I really do love her.

"Kia, I'm sorry for everything. Truly, I am." I want to be as sincere as possible. Kia scoots closer to me to hold my hand. She apologizes as I lay my head on her shoulder. We sit together for a few moments and she invites me to stay the night. I accept her offer, and she goes run me a hot bath. I dread to see what I looked like. My head is pounding, my eye burns, my stomach is doing somersaults and I have probably five or so bricks in my damn car. Rest is much needed after the night I just had.

Awkwardly, Kia caters to my every need. I don't know how many female friendships would survive after the WWII she and I just experienced. I imagine it's because we are both humble. Humble enough to know when to right our wrongs. I can't prove whether Derrick had something to do with Michael being almost murdered, but I can take initiative and inform my husband that I have been having an affair. Hopefully, he's still willing to go to counseling and continue with our marriage.

I ease into the hot bath water and plan how I'm

going to break the news to Michael. Should I tell him the next time I'm at the hospital or maybe I should wait until he comes home? Either way, I'm ready to come clean about my affair and move forward with my husband.

TWENTY-THREE

ALMOST THREE MONTHS LATER...

I'm now finally home, with therapy sessions of course. It's been a long journey but I'm still here, and I couldn't ask for anything more. Ashley just graduated with her Ph.D. and is about to start her practice. She's also obtained her LCPC, Licensed Clinical Professional Counselor. I couldn't be more ecstatic for her. Things are looking better for us; especially since we just found out we are having a baby. She's only five weeks, which is still pretty early; however, we are both extremely excited. In between my intense physical therapy sessions, our counseling sessions were even more intense. She

227

never mentioned she had an affair but always had thoughts of having one. She only admitted to falling out of love with me. I've tried to reignite our relationship by being more spontaneous, but Ashley is too busy for me. So our marriage counselor gave us homework every time we've left the office.

One of our biggest assignments was to get to know each other all over again. You never realize how much a person can change and grow during the course of the relationship. It was little things that I wasn't aware of. All this time I thought Ashley's favorite color was pink; now it's purple! She actually hates going to the movies; I thought she enjoyed it, but she would only go to the show to please me. So we agreed to go on dates every weekend. We take walks in the park; well, not long walks. I'm still not able to walk longer than ten minutes without pain. We've started creating new memories by trying different things, like going to the museum, body painting—just to name a few. Honestly, I enjoy the new life and memories that we are trying to create especially with this new baby coming soon.

Everything is going in a positive direction. Sean and I are closer than ever before, Kia and Ashley are on great terms. I still don't know why Kia kicked her ass so bad. No one really told me the true reason behind their fight. You know how when you enter a room and you can sense that everyone is talking about you? Well, same scenario. I can feel that everyone knows something but are refusing to inform me. Nonetheless, it's the past, and I'm just trying to move on. My company is doing better than ever. We've picked up four major clients since I was hospitalized. I still remember the first day I returned to work and what a surprise it was.

"Surprise! Welcome back!" I could hear the loud chants from everyone in the office as they each greeted me. There were all sorts of foods, desserts, drinks, and chips spread out on a long table. My office was decorated with welcome back balloons and flowers. I was presented with gifts ranging from a gift card to a Rolex watch that I received from a former client. I didn't think anything else could make me smile any harder until I was presented with four different contracts. It's an overwhelming feeling to have contracts in my hand. It lets me know that not only my company is trusted, but my company will be in business for at least two to three years per contract. It also pays to have a solid team who can hold down the fort when you're not around. I'm forever grateful for that.

"Babe, are you ready?" Ashley interrupts my thoughts as she rushes down the stairs. We have an appointment with her OBGYN to hear the heartbeat and to make sure everything is okay with the baby. When we went to the emergency room last month, we thought Ashley just had the flu. That's when we discovered there was a baby. The ER nurse told us to follow up with her primary OB, and that's what we are doing today.

"Yes, let me grab my shoes. Did you want to stop for lunch afterward? I wanted to try that new sushi place on the corner of Lark Avenue."

"Yuck! Just the smell of that makes me nauseous again!" She makes those annoying gagging sounds, showing how overly dramatic she really is.

"Fine. We can go wherever you want. Ready?" I open the front door for Ashley then collide against her back as she stops dead in her tracks when a red Bentley cruises past our house.

"Who is that, babe?" I question, but she doesn't respond. She stares until the car is no longer visible. There's something vaguely familiar about that car, I just can't put my finger on it.

We finally make it to the doctors. The nurse weighs Ashley in and takes all the necessary vitals. She explains the doctor is running forty minutes behind on schedule, but for Ashley to strip down, get comfortable, and wait. Seeing Ashley naked completely turns me on, so before she is able to put on her smock, I sit her down and spread her legs. I just want to please her, so I spread her thighs and suck her lips, pleasing her until she orgasms twice. I could keep going, but I don't want to lose track of time. I definitely don't want to risk the doctor walking in on us.

"Oh my God, baby, what was that for? she flirts after I stand and cover her.

Just want to make you happy, baby, that's all." There's a brief pause in the room. I'm sure she knows that all I ever want to do is make her happy.

"I will always love you, Michael. Thank you for being so amazing to me. I couldn't ask for a better husband. God must really love me to bless me with someone like you."

Those words are like music to my ears and it feels good to know that she feels the same way about me that I feel about her.

There's a knock on the door and we invite the doctor into the room. She asks Ashley a couple of questions before telling her to lay back on the bed to perform a breast exam. I honestly don't know what is going on with my hormones, but observing the doctor rubbing and feeling on Ashley's breast makes me rock hard. After she's finished with the breast exam, she props my wife's legs up so that she can do a vaginal exam. The doctor sits between her legs and brings the light that is adjoined to the bed closer to Ashley's vagina. Then the doctor laughs.

"Well, I guess we don't need any lubrication now, do we?"

"Oh sorry. It was a forty-minute wait, if you know what I mean!" Ashley is clearly embarrassed.

The doctor takes a quick glance at me, and I return her glance with a wink and a smirk. I have to make it known that I'm the man.

She continues the vaginal exam by using a long Q-tip and performs a cervical exam by inserting two fingers inside her vagina. If this doesn't turn any man on, I don't know what would. Now it's time for my favorite part, the ultrasound. I can't wait to hear the fierce sounds of his or her heartbeat. The doctor squirts the ultrasound gel on my wife's tummy. I stand up to grab her hand.

"There it is! We found the heartbeat!" the doctor joyfully says after a minute or so of searching. Our baby is so tiny, too tiny, to have a heartbeat as powerful as the one I'm hearing. My heart is filled with so much joy that I begin to weep. I've always wanted children, especially since I was stripped of my family.

"Is there any chance she could be having twins? The nurse at the E.R said she's five weeks. Even though the baby looks small, it doesn't look like what a five-week embryo should look like, according to Google," I challenge.

"Five weeks? She's definitely not five weeks. I'm doing the measurements now, and it looks like you are about fifteen or so weeks pregnant. Your due date is October 27th. I'm going to send for more tests because you are still fairly underweight," she tells Ashley.

I notice the shift in Ashley's aura. She isn't as excited as she was before. I squeeze her hand tightly, letting her know that I'm always going to be here for her. Maybe she got nervous when the doctor expressed her concern about Ashley being underweight.

"You mentioned twins... do twins run in either one of your families?" The doctor leaves the question open to anyone to answer.

"Yeah, I have a fraternal twin, but we were separated at birth. I've never had the chance to meet him. I have no idea if he's alive or deceased. All I know for certain is that my mom and dad are both deceased," I reveal.

"Oh, I'm sorry to hear that. But just to put it out there, there's only one baby in the oven." She giggles as she wipes the gel from my wife's stomach, then she prints out an ultrasound picture for a keepsake.

The doctor tells Ashley to dress then she'll see her in six weeks for a follow-up appointment. After scheduling with reception, we make our way to the car with Ashley quiet as a church mouse. I'm not sure what's going through her head, but whatever it is weighs heavily on the both of us.

We drive to the nearest burger spot since we

both have a taste for burgers and fries. I want to get some insight as to why the sudden mood change.

"Something is bothering you, what is it?"

"Nothing, love, I'm just nervous about having a baby. What if I'm not a good mother; what if I disappoint you and the baby. What if..."

"Are you being facetious right now? How can you not see how amazing you are? You are a wonderful wife, and you are going to be a better mother."

She smiles and leans in for a kiss.

"I could kiss you right now." Ashley smiles with confidence.

"Then come and give me one." I meet her halfway across our table until our lips touch.

Our food comes just in time because my stomach is singing louder than Ke-Ke Wyatt. We continue our small talk.

CLOSER THAN YOU THINK

"What do you think we are having? Wait, we never asked the doctor if it was a boy or girl babe." It completely slips my mind to ask questions.

"That's fine. I actually don't want to know until the baby gets here. I want it to be a surprise for both of us. I think that will be exciting, don't you? She grins.

"Baby, at this point, it's whatever you want. I just want to keep that smile on your beautiful face." I was interrupted when I notice that same candy apple Bentley pull up. The driver and I catch each other's eye before he pulls off. There is something vaguely reminiscent to what I've seen before. It's like I know him from somewhere, but can't pinpoint where.

We finish our lunch and decide to catch a movie. Of course, we can't agree on which one so we decide to just walk in and whatever is playing at the time is what we will see. Everything is going great until Ashley's phone starts vibrating off the hook. Usually when her phone does that, it's not work. I've been in the know long enough to decipher between work and pleasure.

"Hold on, baby, let me take this call," she whispered as she walks out of the show.

"Yep, of course," I respond nonchalantly. This behavior is nothing new to me. Even though it has subsided, I have a strange feeling it's about to return with a vengeance. Something deep down inside tells me that whoever who was in that Bentley has something to do with Ashley running out of the show and me having this uneasy feeling. I wish I had full recollection of what happened prior to the day I was shot. How is it that I can vividly remember the feeling of Ashley having an affair but can't recall shit about that almost deadly night. I don't even remember going to the gym. It's crazy the different memories your brain chooses to store.

It's almost twenty minutes before she returns to her seat next to me. I try to mask the irritation but, apparently, I can't.

"Let's go now!" I demand.

"Wait, why? The movie just started. Plus I want to see it," she whines.

"Look, I'm tired and frustrated. I need to go home and get some rest. Besides, my lower back is beginning to bother me." I make up that excuse so I don't have to be in her presence much longer.

"What has gotten into you? We were just fine a couple minutes ago. Sometimes you come off as being bipolar. I never know with you," she scolds.

We are now standing outside the theater, giving customers a quick show. It's evident I'm highly pissed off. She makes me more upset when she pretends to be oblivious to her actions.

"You want to know what's bothering me? You! Right now, you are bothering me! You honestly believe I don't know what's going on? Huh? Matter of fact, who was that on the phone? And you better not say work because I know that's a damn lie," I hiss.

"Are you kidding me right now?" she responds. I walk away, knowing she couldn't answer that question honestly. Our drive on the way home is quiet. I text Sean and ask if it's okay if I stop by. He says of course and he will drop me off at the house later. Sean and Kia live only five minutes away from us. My vibe is totally off. I've lost the desire to do everything our therapist suggested that we should do when we start to feel uneasy. Ashley knows damn well why I'm upset. There's no need to communicate that to her. The only thing I say to her is to drop me off at Sean's house.

"What's up? It's good to see you, bro!" Sean greets me with a hug as I enter his residence.

"It's good to see you too!" I rebut.

I follow Sean to the kitchen where he grabs a six-pack of Miller Lite. I greet Kia with a kiss on the cheek and ask for her to save me a taco. She has the house smelling like a Mexican fiesta. We head downstairs to the basement.

"What's going on, have a seat! Do you want a beer?" That really isn't a question because he doesn't give me an opportunity to answer. He's pretty much shoving the beer down my damn throat.

"I hate that I can't remember shit, bro. Something is going on, and I feel like everyone knows except for me!" I snap.

"Something like what?"

"Something is going on with Ashley, and I know you know."

Sean looks dead at me and doesn't say a word. That's all the confirmation I need.

"First, tell me what happened for you to think something is going on with Ashley."

I sigh, sit back on the sofa, and tell him the specifics of what occurred today.

"As we were leaving to go see her doctor, there was a red Bentley that drove down our street. I didn't think shit of it; I figured maybe they were looking for an address or something. Then, Ashley stood frozen in her tracks as she stared at the car until it disappeared from our view. You know I had to ask her what happened, and she didn't say shit. The crazy thing about it was that car was very familiar, but I don't know anyone who drives a Bentley. Then, we get to the diner and that same car pulled into the parking lot as Ashley and I watched from our window seat inside the diner. That same weird feeling came back over me. I saw the guy behind the wheel and I swear I knew him from somewhere, but I just don't know where. I know this all sounds preposterous, but I'm not tripping… I'm not losing my mind."

"Look, there's something I need to tell you. Do you have any memory of the day that you were followed?" The seriousness in his voice has me spooked.

"No… Wait, someone was following me?"

"Well, I don't know if it was the same car or not, but the car that followed you to the gas station and all the way to our church was a red Bentley. It's not a coincidence that you feel some type of way. Your brain is probably trying to help you recall the memory that you've lost."

"For whatever reason, I have a strong sense that getting shot wasn't an accident. More importantly, I believe my incident had some connection to Ashley. I don't think she had me set up or anything; I just feel as if she's involved one way or another," I express with sadness.

Sean rapidly becomes stricken with sorrow. This further let me know he knows something that I don't. I don't even give him a chance to respond. I become so enraged at the thought of him withholding secrets from me.

"What the hell do you freaking know?" I hiss.

"I really don't know a damn thing while you're snapping at me. I can only assume the same car that followed you about seven months ago was probably the same car you saw today. Don't take your anger out on me; save that shit for Ashley! That's who you're really pissed at. I haven't said shit to you because I don't have any concrete facts, only assumptions. I've been your best friend for years so if I'm going to bring anything to you, it will be facts ONLY!" He emphasizes *only.*

"Sorry, man. You're right. I'm taking my shit out on you instead of Ashley, where it belongs. Let's just start over. I just need to get this off my chest and I don't know how to broach the topic with her." I rebut.

I relax a little. Plus, he's right. I'm not mad at him, I'm mad at Ashley. I hate having this feeling all the damn time, and I hate more that I took some of my aggression out Sean. I immediately apologize and ask if we can just start over.

"Man, we all think Ashley is or was having an affair, but none of us have proof. I've asked Kia, but I can't expect her to rat out her girl. Did she admit to her cheating during your counseling sessions?"

"No. All she said was that she had thoughts of cheating but she never did."

"Okay, there you have it! I'm not about to put any bugs in your ear about your wife. What's done in the dark will come to light, especially if it's meant for you to find out."

"You're right. This is just too much! It's driving me completely insane."

"Mike, you're giving this situation way too much power over you. Trust me when I say, if it's meant for you to find out, you will. Now let's dead this conversation and tell me about my nephew," he cackles.

I need to release all this negative energy quick. Ashley and I have come so far in our marriage for us to resort back to where we were prior. I need to get healthy and stay healthy, both mentally and physically for the sake of our child.

"I hope it's a boy, but so far so good. I left the ultrasound in the car but the baby's heartbeat is strong as an ox. We did find out she's further along than we thought, so that's a good thing. Her due date is in October."

"Are you excited? Shit, I am! My nephew will be the closest thing I have to a son," Sean sadly expresses.

"You know you are more than welcome to come to the house anytime. Besides, you can babysit every weekend too," I reassure. I know how much he wants children, but will never experience fatherhood due to the accident Kia was in years ago.

"I'm going to hold you to that," Kia replies, eavesdropping on our conversation. She has two plates in her hand, both filled with chicken tacos, Mexican rice, and guacamole. I wasn't serious when I asked her to save me a taco, I was just trying to make small talk as I greeted her. In spite of me not being hungry, I still eat the meal she prepared for me.

It isn't long after that my stomach starts rumbling. I don't feel comfortable having a bowel movement in someone else's house. Besides, I still need help transitioning from the toilet to standing up. That I haven't mastered yet. Therefore, I ask Sean if he can drop me off at home.

We pull in front of my home, and I don't see Ashley's car parked in our driveway. I figure she may have parked her car in the garage instead. I walked in, anxious to talk to her about how I'm feeling, but she's nowhere to be found. It doesn't even look like she came home. I grab my cell phone from my jacket to call her. No answer! Here we go again!

TWENTY-FOUR

I had Ashley on her knees giving me the best head I've ever had. I'm completely disgusted by this bitch. All this time she's been telling me her husband was still in a coma when he's been home. She quickly ran over to my house after she saw my homeboy ride past her home. Little does she know, I knew about her husband being home way before that. I'll just continue to play the dummy until she tells me the truth. I'm waiting for her to come clean about her being pregnant. I'm also aware of their doctor's appointment this morning. My cousin is the receptionist at the office. It didn't take my cousin much to access her records after I sent her $200 through her Cash App. I'm not going to force Ashley to bring up the pregnancy. Maybe the baby isn't mine. We did have a two-week drought so now that I know her husband has been alive and well, maybe it's his. Or shit, maybe she's about to abort the motherfucker; who knows.

She can't even make me come anymore. I have to think of my next-door neighbor that I've been sleeping with in order to orgasm. Ashley opens her mouth as wide as she can so she doesn't miss a drop. After I release everything I have into her mouth, I tell her to leave. She's devastated, but I don't give a fuck. I've lost all respect for her, but if she's willing to still give me some ass then that's on her. Throughout all these years, I've been nothing but good and faithful to her. I've always been honest, and I even wanted to marry her. She lied to me by not revealing that she was married. I'm a victim too. Then to find out he was supposedly beating on her; I did what I thought was best to protect her. I wonder if that was a lie as well. Everything that comes out of her mouth is a lie.

"Damn, that's where we are now? You're going

to kick me out of your house after I suck your dick?" Ashley screams as she wipes my semen from her chin.

"Yep! Now get the hell out!"

"Fuck you, bitch! You ain't shit and you will never be shit!" She slams my door so damn hard that the glass shatters. She's lucky that I'm getting that door replaced this weekend anyway.

I open my laptop to respond to some emails. I have my first showing next weekend, and I'm a nervous wreck. I've always wanted to get into real estate, and I 'm happy now that I have my license. My new friend, Sasha, has helped me tremendously throughout this process. Sasha is a sweet girl, but so was Ashley at first; I'll definitely keep my guard up. It was when she offered to pay for me to take my real estate exam that made me lower the wall that I built around me. Of course, I denied her offering. Sasha's beautiful. She's very much different than Ashley. Sasha is five-feet-ten, semi chubby, her skin as dark as cocoa but smooth as silk. Her smile is contagious, and she has the energy and the confidence to match. Men are naturally drawn to her; I'm one of them.

We had our first date about two months ago. Since we live a couple houses down from each other, she met me at my car. As soon as I walked outside and saw her standing near my car, I couldn't take my eyes off her. Normally I wouldn't date a chubby girl, but she carries her weight well and she's secure in her skin. She has cheekbones like Janet Jackson that make their debut every time she smiles. We had a great time that night, probably the best time I've ever had with anyone. She's the first girl that I didn't desire to be sexual with right away. I truly wanted to get to know more about her. Her secrets, her fears, her happy place, her favorite color... I'm so intrigued by this woman. Although my plan was to take her right back home, she ended up at my place for a nightcap. We made love and I held on to her all night. I didn't want her to leave the next morning. I woke up to breakfast in bed before she departed. I don't think Ashley ever made me breakfast in bed; I'd usually cook for her.

Sasha has been my backbone for the last two months. I was honest with her about Ashley, and she was extremely understanding. Don't get me wrong, I still love Ashley but I'm not in love with her anymore. The abundant amount of lies has completely made me dislike her. I knew this relationship between Ash and me wasn't going to last too long, and I promised Sasha that I was going to end it soon.

I'm exhilarated at the idea of starting a new life with Sasha and my new life as a real estate agent. I'm tired of hustling, making my money the illegal way. I have enough saved to start my own real estate management firm, and Sasha will be right there by my side. We've already started working on my business plan and my goals. I've created a vision board and it's the best thing I could've done. I'm appreciative that she advised me to do so.

My cell phone vibrates and I walk over to the counter where it lay. It's Ashley on FaceTime. I instantly decline her call. It doesn't matter because she calls back right away, so I decline it again. This cat and mouse game continued for another three minutes until I decided to block her ass. I'll eventually unblock her but, as for now, I need to be unbothered for a little while.

Since I have my phone in my hand, I send Tommy a text and ask him to meet me at my house. I have a serious bone to pick with him; he' was becoming sloppy at his job. He fucked up by not finishing what he started, but now he's risking being seen by Ashley's husband. Granted, Michael has some form of amnesia, but one day he may just regain his memory and I can't risk that. There's only one thing that has to be done at this point; Tommy has to go. I can't trust him enough to not rat me out. Plus, there's talk around town that Tommy shot Michael. I've never opened my mouth so that only means Tommy's mouth was running. I hate that it has gotten to this point but, as I mentioned before, Tommy is too sloppy. If Ashley didn't already assume that Tommy and I had something to do with the shooting of her husband, I'm sure she knows something now. It's not a coincidence that she texted me after she left the burger joint or while she was at the movies. Therefore, I have to eliminate the problem…Tommy.

Tommy's in the area and arrives at my house within five minutes. I put the silencer on my SIG Sauer P226 and sit it on the ledge. Unbeknownst to Tommy, tonight will be his last night breathing. One thing I've learned living this life is to be careful of those who have nothing to lose. Tommy doesn't have anything, just the spare change I gave him for the work that needed to be done.

This isn't the first time Tommy's been careless. Years ago, he fucked up a drug deal so bad I lost over $500,000. He didn't listen to my detailed instructions, took the wrong bag, and showed up at the wrong place. Because of that, the Cubans who I was trying to establish a solid business with decided to do business elsewhere. The Cubans were pushing enough weight that my great, great, great grandchildren would've been set for life. I wanted to be part of that, and it took me over a year to finally meet with their team. Part of me blamed myself for not being there, but Tommy was adamant about showing how valuable he was to me. I wanted to trust that he would do the right thing, so I sent a boy to do a man's job; it backfired. Luckily, I didn't have a war on my hands, and the Cubans only decided to wash all ties with me. Things could've been worse as I could've had a hit out on me. They were notorious for the astronomical amount of bloodshed to those who crossed them. Even though I was about that life too, my army wasn't as strong or deep as his.

I open the door, and Tommy is high as shit. His eyes are bloodshot red and his pupils are dilated. He uses his sleeve to wipe his nose repeatedly. It doesn't take me long to realize that he's using my products again. For that reason alone, I need to end his life. He's no asset to me. He's the reason I had Ashley take the rest of my stash and hide it in her home. I knew if I ever got busted, her place would be the last the cops would think to search.

"Follow me downstairs." I signal to Tommy as I walk toward my basement. Old, thick sheets cover the couches and the floors so blood wouldn't stain them.

"What's all of this? You remodeling again?" he questions hesitantly.

"Yeah, something like that!" He knows what's about to go down. My heart softens for a spilt second, but immediately hardens at the thought of everything he has done. I think about the amount of money I've spent on him in and out of rehab, the money I lost with the Cubans. I thought about how he couldn't even complete the job with Ashley's husband. How flashy he is in that stupid bright red ass Bentley. I grab the pistol and point directly at his skull. Immediate fear overcomes his body as urine seeps through his pants.

"Yo, yo... what's all this about? What are you doing?" he yells as he stands frozen with his hands in the air.

"I'm sorry. I love you."

I close my eyes as I hear the last words, "No, wait... wait," exit his mouth before I pull the trigger. My eyes remain closed as I hear his body slump onto the floor. Tears quickly fall from my eyes. I truly did love Tommy, and he was the closest thing to a brother to me. I was the only child before I left home, and I gained a brother in Tommy in the streets. I remind myself that this was necessary and I had no choice. My mind is convinced that I've done the right thing but my heart overshadows my thoughts. I instantly feel regretful as I rush near Tommy's side. He lay there, completely lifeless. I touch his eyes to close them shut. I plant a kiss on his forehead and mutter, "I'm sorry, brother." I wrap his body in the sheets that I placed out before he arrived. I take his cell phone, wallet, and keys and place them in my fire pit that's lit outside. I grab a couple of ropes from the backyard and place one around his neck, waist, and feet. I make sure the ropes are secure enough that I won't drop him once I drape his body around my shoulder. I look outside to make sure no one is looking. I'm not worried because my privacy fence stands seven feet. I walk toward my garage and place him in the trunk. Blood seeps through the sheets so I get another sheet from the garage and triple tie it around his head. I drive to my warehouse where I have my own crematory services for this very reason hidden deep in the back. I open the door to the furnace and the heat blazes as I throw Tommy inside. I stand in disbelief and watch what's left of Tommy perish.

TWENTY-FIVE

THREE MONTHS LATER...

I scream at the top of my lungs, begging whoever to take this damn baby out of me. Just a week ago, I was attending my baby shower and now, I'm in labor. I don't know why I went into labor early, but this baby is coming. We don't know the sex of the baby, we all want it to be a surprise. My baby shower was amazing, and we had a huge turnout. We had over 100 attendees and received over 200 gifts including those who were in attendance and from those who couldn't make it. I was overwhelmed with the amount of love I received. Life with Michael couldn't have been better. I hadn't heard from Derrick in months, and I eventually stopped trying to reach out to him. The way he treated me the last time we were together broke me. He treated me like I was a piece of shit. I've always treated him like royalty, but I received the short end of the stick. I even heard that he was dating some new chick now; actually, I didn't hear that. I saw it with my own eyes. I stalked him for about a month after he blocked me and learned that his neighbor was his lover.

"Please! Somebody! I need drugs! Give me some drugs please!" I continue to plead. My contractions are becoming stronger and stronger and I'm becoming weaker by the minute. I'm only three centimeters dilated so therefore they can't administer any drugs until I'm at four centimeters. Michael holds my hand and rubs my back as I cry out in agony. How in the hell could any woman say they would do this over again?

"Here comes another contraction, Ash. Get ready." Michael prepped me for the pain I'm about to endure for thirty seconds.

I buckle down and brace for the impact! This contraction is worse than the last ones.

"Ahhhhh... I can't take this... Please make this pain stop." It feels like Satan is crushing every bone in my body. Then he'll put me back together only to crush them again.

"Page the nurse. I can't take another one of these contractions, baby," I beg. I'm sweating profusely, and I'm extremely tired. No one believes me when I plead that I'm not feeling well. I'm weak due to the intense contractions but something else is going on.

There nurse walks in and I try to explain what I'm feeling before the next contraction hits, but I don't make it. I'm not sure what happened, but I woke up panicked and disoriented. I look around the room and try to familiarize myself with my surroundings.

"Oh my God, where's my baby, Kia?" I panic as I touched my stomach.

"Calm down! He's fine. He's in N.I.C.U, but he's okay. They had to do an emergency C-Section. You had some internal bleeding and passed out. Good news is they were able to save your ovaries and the baby. Bad news is, you're going to have an ugly ass scar for life," she laughs.

Hearing the word, 'he's' makes me tear up. I just had a beautiful baby boy. Michael and I already decided that if the baby was a boy, we would name him Michael Jr, MJ for short.

"Where's Michael?"

"Oh, he's with the baby," Kia explains. She pages the nurse and gives me some water that was left on the bedside table for me. I try to reach for the tissue, but the lower part of my body is still numb. I assume it's from the anesthesia; otherwise, I believe Kia would've told me something different.

"Hi, you're awake! How are you feeling?" the chipperly nurse askes.

"I feel okay. I just want to see my baby. Can I

see him?"

"Of course, you can. Let me go get a wheelchair. We'll get you situated, and I can take you to see your son. He's perfect. You're going to fall in love with him."

That makes my heart smile. I can't wait to hold him, to smell him, to kiss him. I'm already in love with him, and I haven't officially met him yet.

No more than two minutes pass before the nurse returns with the wheelchair. Another nurse comes in to assist as they help me into the chair. I thought I was numb but as soon as I sit up completely, I feel every staple that is stitched into my skin. Kia follows closely as I ride in silence to the N.I.C.U. There are so many babies, some so small that they likely won't make it. Others attached to breathing machines. I see Michael standing, holding our son.

When he sees me being rolled closer to him, he smiles. There's my baby, perfect as he could possibly be.

"Here's our son!" Michael says as he gently hands the baby to me. I can't stop the tears from flowing. Now I see why women say they would go through this process all over again. It's for this very moment. The first moment you and your baby lock eyes. I know he knows who I am; I can see the warmness in his eyes. He stares at me and I stare back with a smile.

"I love you, MJ," I whisper and plant a kiss on his cheek.

"Were you interested in breastfeeding?" the nurse asks.

"Yes, can I feed him now?"

"Let's wait until we can get your temperature down, then we can bring you in to feed him."

I completely ignore the doctor informing me of my temperature. She even suggests that I get some much-needed rest so that I can actually feed my son the next day, but I don't want to leave MJ's side. I feel like I'll miss something if I do.

Three hours pass and I'm still sitting in the wheelchair holding MJ. I was able to feed him with the small bottle they gave us. The doctor stopped by to check my stitches and my temperature.

"You really need to lay down and get some rest. If you want to get better, you have to listen to what we tell you, Mrs. Williams," the doctor mentions.

"I can't leave my baby. Is there any way I can just stay here?" I suggest.

"How about we do this… I'll see if we can get you a private room right next to the N.I.C.U. That way you are near your son and you can get comfortable so you can rest. I'm more concerned with your health. Your temperature is 104.6. It's been high over six hours."

I can hear the concern in his voice and it doesn't help that Michael has now voiced his opinion. I finally agree to get a room next to the N.I.C.U. I don't feel sick; I'm on a natural high. I'm overly thrilled about this bundle of joy laying in his incubator. He's all that matters and nothing else.

It doesn't take long, perhaps an hour, to get a room made for me. I understand their concern so I decide to rest while Michael stays with the baby. MJ looks just like his daddy. He has his daddy's nose and long chin. It's obvious that he has my full lips. I grin, pondering all the good things I have planned for MJ. I even smile at the idea of Michael and I eventually being grandparents one day. As much as I think about the future and how wonderful things will be, I can't help but to revert back to the life I had with Derrick. I know Derrick should be the last thing on my mind, but I'm still deeply in love with him. I grab my cell phone and hurry to send a text before I completely doze off. The medication is kicking in that the nurses put in my I.V.

"Hey. I don't want anything. I just want to tell you that I still love you, and I'm sorry for everything. FYI, I had a beautiful healthy boy today. Take care."

I don't wait to see if he texts back. I doze off, thrilled at the idea that I'm not blocked from his phone. I see that my message was delivered. Even if he doesn't reply, he now knows that I do love him and that I'm apologetic for everything.

TWENTY-SIX

I sit at church with my family and closest friends. MJ is four-months-old and today we are having him christened. Sean is his godfather, of course, and Kia is appointed his godmother. Ashley's parents drove all the way from Illinois to share this special occasion with us. They will be in town, staying with us for the next two weeks.

Service is going great, as usual. The pastor is going to call us up after alter call. Ashley excuses herself to the bathroom and lays MJ in my arms as she leaves the service. The trust I have for Ash has diminished. I never questioned Ashley about the text I saw from a guy name Derrick when she was in the hospital. I didn't actually see what was said, but I saw his name across her phone screen when I went to check on her. It doesn't bother me that another man texts my wife. It's the fact he has a heart emoji behind his name that strikes a chord with me. I know all of Ashley's friends and the majority of her male co-workers, but I've never met anyone named Derrick. We put a halt on our therapy sessions because we couldn't fit it in our schedules anymore, so she said. I found that hilarious because Ashley still manages to find time to do whatever she wants to do. I've ignored a lot, but I haven't been oblivious to the fact that Ashley was an adulterer. MJ gives me peace and keeps me sane.

"This is one of my favorite parts of the service. This is when we give our children to God. Being baptized represents the cleansing of sin. Psalm 51:5 says, 'Behold, I was brought forth in iniquity, and in sin my mother conceived me.' We are living in a world where our babies are being murdered and raped by the hands of their own mothers. Sin is all around us—in our homes, in our churches, in our jobs. The job of the parents and the godparents is to protect their children. The first step is offering their children to God…"

My pastor preaches about the importance of having a child in the church. I turn around to search for Ashley, but she's nowhere to be seen. I mouth the words, 'Where's Ashley?' to one of the ushers who stand near the exit. Two minutes later, Ashley slides into the pew right before the pastor calls the family up for MJ.

The christening ceremony lasts fifteen minutes or less. Pastor acknowledges the godparents and advises them of the importance of their roles. Then he offers my son to God, and the congregation joins us in prayer.

We gather after service where everyone offers congratulations and blessings for MJ. It feels good to know that I have the saints in the church praying for my family and me. There was a time when Ashley was told that I might not survive, but all praises are due to the Most High. I glance around to see if I can spot Ashley. I eventually catch a glimpse of her speaking to a person that I've never seen before. I make my way to introduce myself, but I'm sidetracked by more church members who want to offer their blessings. By the time I make it over, the gentleman is gone and Ashley is waiting at the door for me, along with Sean and Kia.

"Let's all go out for dinner?" Kia suggests.

"Yeah, that sounds like a plan! I have a taste for a steak. What about Morton's?" Sean mentions.

"I'm down for that, what about you, baby?" Ashley asks.

"I'm okay with that, but can I talk to you for a second?" I tell Kia and Sean that we will meet them outside then pull Ashley aside. We all rode together to church this morning. It didn't make sense to drive two separate vehicles when we all were going to the same place.

"What's going on, baby?" Ashley whispers.

"Who was that man you were talking to a few minutes ago?"

"What man? You have to be more specific than that, honey. There were tons of men who talked to me today. I…"

"Cut the bull crap, Ashley! You know darn well what man I'm talking about. I know every man in this church, and I've never seen that guy," I snap while cutting her completely off. She's hiding something because she has a tendency to start rambling and providing unnecessary information.

"If you're referring to the guy in that red shirt, his name is Derrick. He's a patient of mine. That's it, nothing more nothing less." Her stern voice doesn't sit well with me. She grabs MJ from my arms so she can calm him down. He was becoming antsy, perhaps because he was hungry.

"So when did we start inviting our patients to private family affairs?" I ask, totally forgetting that this is the same man with a heart emoji saved by his name in her cell phone.

"Can we have this conversation some other time? You're making this to be a bigger deal than what it is. He's a patient, that's it!" Ashley walks off with MJ in her arms. I grab the diaper bag that she left on the pew and meet up with her outside.

Sean has an Infiniti truck that seats seven passengers which is perfect because I don't want to sit anywhere near Ashley. For that reason alone, I sit in the very back row while Ashley sits in the middle row with MJ. She securely straps him in his car seat, and we ride in silence to Morton's restaurant up the street.

After dinner, Sean drops us off at home. I'm ready to finish our conversation. I've been quiet for too long. That Derrick guy is more than just a patient, her body language said otherwise. I can't wait to hear the rumors that will be circulating soon. Any blind person could see there was something more going on. I wait until she puts MJ in his crib and closes the door.

"You ready to talk now?" I ask as I follow her into our bedroom. She removes her clothes and dresses into something more comfortable. I do the same.

"It's nothing to talk about! You're overreacting as usual. He's my fucking patient! What more do you want me to say?" Ashley retorts.

"Who the hell do you think you're talking to in my house, woman? I pay the damn bills in here! If I'm not raising my voice at you, you damn sure aren't going to raise your voice at me!"

"Your house? Last time I checked, this house is in my damn name, not yours! Remember how sucky your credit was? It's because of me that we even have this house, so I can raise my damn voice any time I please."

"Woman, please, I didn't have any credit... that's the difference! And let's not talk about credit scores now when you're one step away from filing bankruptcy!"

By now, we're both in a yelling match, neither one of us talking about the matter at hand. How we get on the topic about credit scores and credit cards is beyond me. The fact that she does a great job deflecting from my original question is baffling, almost hilarious.

"Shut up!" I scream at the top of my lungs. It makes Ashley jump in fear and MJ cries out.

"Go take care of my son." I turn my back to her and go to my basement where I sleep for the remainder of the night.

I receive a text from Ashley the next morning informing me that she's about to go to work and that MJ has been fed, cleaned, and put back to sleep. I have my yearly follow up with my doctor today, and I'm excited to show my kid off to everyone in the office. I wasn't expecting breakfast to be made for me, especially after the argument Ashley and I had. But to my amazement, there are pancakes, sausage, and eggs waiting for me. I eat and get dressed because my appointment is in about two hours. I pack

275

MJ's bag because I plan to stop by Sean's house afterward, since he doesn't have to work today.

I wait over an hour to be called into a room at the doctor's office. I'm beyond exhausted and so is MJ. He whined and moaned until I finally got up to walk around with him. That seems like the only thing that soothes his soft cries.

"Oh wow! Who do we have here?" my doctor asks as he enters the room, sixty minutes post-scheduled appointment time. The check-in process is brutal. No one should have to wait this damn long to see a doctor when you've scheduled an appointment weeks in advance.

"This is my son, MJ. Isn't he handsome?" I smile as I introduced MJ to my primary doctor. I even grab his little hand and help him wave 'hello'.

"Your son? Did you guys decide to adopt?" he investigates.

"Adopt? Of course not! Ashley delivered him. We did it the natural way," I laugh.

My doctor looks startled and worried. I'm surely confused by his body language.

"What is it, doctor? You look… confused?"

"I… I'm sorry to even say this… but… um…"

"But um what?"

"There's no way he can be yours. Do you remember me telling you that you were sterile? When you were shot in your upper thigh, there was some severe damage done to your groin area causing sterilization. After running multiple tests, your sperm count is only at one million. The norm is fifteen million."

I don't physically or mentally process anything after he said "There's no way he can be yours." How is that even possible? This boy looks just like me or, at least, that's what everyone says. This has to be a mistake.

"Wait, something isn't right. I don't recall you mentioning anything about my sperm count or you running any tests, Doc!"

"You suffer from amnesia which probably still has some effect on you. I ensure you that I had this conversation with you. You told me that you understood. Do you not have any recollection of us having that conversation?"

"Of course not! Don't you think I would've killed Ashley by now had I remembered?" I growl. I stand up to calm MJ down who is startled by my outburst.

"Let me get the paperwork so that you can see for yourself. I wouldn't lie to you, I promise. Especially with something like this," he rebuts.

I sit down, infuriated at the thought that MJ may not be mine. I grab his bottle from the bag and place it in his mouth. I wait for the doctor to search through my records on his computer, but I have a better idea.

"Can you schedule a DNA test for me right now since I'm here?"

The doctor turns to me with a sorrowful look plastered on his face.

"If that's what you truly want, I can get that scheduled for you right now."

"Yes, that's what I want," I firmly state.

"I'll get it ordered now. I'll be back in a second and again, I do apologize. I honestly thought you knew. I didn't mean to be the bearer of bad news."

"It's not your fault; it's the whore ass wife of mine."

I wait for another twenty minutes before the nurse walks in with some paperwork for me to take to the blood center.

I feel as if I'm walking the green mile to my death. I stare at MJ, praying that he is mine. Ashley knew how much starting a family meant to me and if this was stripped away from me, I honestly can't say what I would do to her.

They call my name as soon as I'm checked in. I

enter the back room where they swabbed both of our mouths and they also take some blood from me. They don't draw any blood from MJ because they have some blood samples from him at birth.

"We will give you a call in about a week or so with the results, or would you prefer that we mail it to your address on file?" the lab technician suggests.

"No, actually, can you guys just give me a call?"

"Sure. No problem. Take care, and we will talk in a couple of days."

I grab MJ's diaper bag and walk to the nearest bathroom so that I can change his pamper. There's no way this kid couldn't be mine. He has the same birthmark on his lower abdomen as I do. I'm infuriated at the idea of getting this bloodwork done. I'm disgusted at myself for even letting that damn doctor convince me that MJ couldn't possibly be mine. He doesn't know how my God operates. I believe in miracles and that anything can happen. I make a prompt decision to cancel the DNA results. I search for the technician, but I don't see him anywhere. Actually, there's no one in the front that I can talk to. I wait a couple of minutes and still, there's no one. I finally leave; forgetting my original appointment, and tell myself that when they call, I won't answer. MJ is my son, and that's all that matters.

TWENTY-SEVEN

It isn't a secret that something is going on between Mike and Ash. The tension is so thick between them after the christening that you could cut it with a knife. It also isn't a coincidence that my wife and Ashley had a fist fight a while back. Knowing my wife, she must have called Ashley out on her shit and, knowing Ashley, she wasn't having it. I understand there's a girl code that my wife adheres to; however, she was friends with Michael before she became friends with Ashley so her loyalty should lie with Michael. I believe Kia knows more than what she's telling me. I even caught a glimpse of Kia looking at the man that was at church talking to Ashley. I knew then that she knew him or knew of him. I try not to pry into anyone's business, especially marital affairs, but Michael is a great man who deserves the best. He doesn't deserve what Ashley is putting him through.

There's a hard knock at my door that completely startles me. One would've thought that the police was at my door, ready to arrest any or everyone inside. I briskly walk to the door so I can curse out whoever is on the other side. I peek through the peephole only to see Michael struggling to hold MJ, his diaper bag, and his car seat. It makes sense that the knocking was done with such force, he was kicking at the door instead. I immediately open the door and grab the first thing that's about to drop… MJ.

"Come in and take a load off," I say as I lift MJ into the air. My godson takes so much joy in me slightly throwing him into the air. All the soft giggles and drool remind me how much he enjoys it.

Michael doesn't say much other than can he grab a water from the fridge. To this day, I still don't understand why he feels the need to ask if he can have anything in my house. I don't respond but give him a look that reminds him to not ask for anything in my house; he's always welcomed to it.

"You okay? What's going on with you?" I probe. It isn't rocket science to know that something is bothering him; it's all over his face.

"I hate bothering you with my problems. I know you're tired of me talking about Ashley." Although I am tired of hearing about her, I would never tell him that. He's my brother, so I will always be here for him.

"You're talking about what happened after service, right?"

"Yeah! You saw that mess, right? Am I tripping or no?" Michael questions.

"No, you're not tripping. I noticed that guy there. Actually, everyone noticed that guy there and how Ashley stayed in his face. It didn't help that he was an attractive man—no homo, though." I make it known that I don't have homosexual tendencies in me.

"I believe that's the guy she's having an affair with. I even confronted her about it when we got home. Nothing was resolved, we ended up arguing about something totally irrelevant," Mike concludes.

I take MJ's bottle out of the bag and place it in his mouth. I secure him in my arms so that he will be comfortable and hopefully fall asleep. I sit across from Michael so that I have his undivided attention.

"You know, a couple weeks ago, I tried to purchase a motorcycle. Only to find out that my credit score dropped tremendously. I couldn't understand why my score was 475. I just knew this had to be a mistake or someone had stolen my identity. I called the credit bureaus and learned that every line of credit that was opened was opened by Kia. We are almost a half of million dollars in debt all because of her."

"Wait, are you being serious right now?" Mike

cuts me off.

"Serious as a heart attack!"

"Have you said anything to her about this? This is a very serious issue! Debt is one of the major causes of divorce."

"No, I haven't said anything to her about it. Nor has she mentioned it to me. It's not like she doesn't know about it. Majority of the credit cards were opened by her over three years ago. Now I see why all the mail goes to her P.O box."

"I know you're not going to let her get away with this! You have to say something to her," he chastises.

"I'm not going to say anything," I add.

"Why not? I don't get it."

"Why should I? I knew what I was getting into when I married her. I knew she had a terrible spending habit and couldn't manage money well. I made that choice to still marry her, faults and all."

Mike doesn't understand where I'm coming from or where I'm going with this story. I continue…

"The moral of my story is, you knew the type of woman she was. You said so yourself. Remember the first night you met her, she was extremely flirtatious with every man at the Christmas party. You had reservations about her then, but you made the ultimate decision to marry her." It's the harsh truth but it's the truth. Ashley is a beautiful woman, and she knows it. She's also the type of woman that makes sure everyone else knows how beautiful she is, even if she has to bend over and throw her ass in your face.

Michael finishes his water and throws the bottle away. He grabs MJ from my arms and secures him in his car seat. Mike, clearly agitated by my remarks, starts to speak.

"I'm about to head out. I will get with you at another time. Take care."

Just that quick, Mike is gone. I don't even get a

chance to apologize. My intentions weren't to hurt his feelings but to bring some awareness to this whole situation. He has to take some responsibility in this. For that reason alone, I haven't mentioned this issue to Kia. I just know how to fight fire with fire, and that's what I wanted to suggest to him. Now it's evident he can't handle the truth. I'll make sure I keep my opinions to myself.

TWENTY-EIGHT

Ashley

I'm still in awe that Derrick had the nerve to show up to my son's christening, even after me warning him not to come. I knew he was only being spiteful because I lied about my husband still being in a coma and he found out the truth. Honestly, I didn't even think he cared about me anymore, so why even cause unnecessary confusion? I know why; it's because he's extremely possessive and a pompous asshole. Despite me being extremely furious with him showing up to my family's event, I couldn't stay away from him. I saw how the women in the church started to gravitate toward him. I had to let all those bitches know that he was off limits even if my husband was sitting on the other side of the church.

"Are you going to suck my dick later?" he continuously texts throughout service.

"I'm in church right now." I try to be discreet as possible so that Michael won't continue to look over my shoulder.

"Yeah, I know. I'm sitting in the back... turn around."

This can't be happening right now. We're about twenty minutes away from the pastor calling the family up to give my only son to God. I pray that Derrick is lying, but a huge part of me knows he is actually sitting in the back. As I peep over my shoulder, Derrick winks at me as he stands up to exit the sanctuary. And that's my cue to follow. I wait two minutes before I act on my thoughts. I send Derrick a text asking where he went. I try not to be so obvious and pretend to be on an important business call while waiting in the hall for Derrick's response.

There's a buzz while I have the phone to my ear, alerting me that I have an incoming text. The text from Derrick asks me to come into the Men's bathroom and that no one is in there. This is wrong and risky, but I just can't say no. I look around, making sure no one is near as I enter the Men's bathroom.

"Derrick?" I whisper.

He opens the second to last stall and pulls me inside. He shoves his tongue down my throat while massaging my breasts. All the respect I have for the house of the Lord and the little respect that I have for my marriage go out the door as I go down on my knees and please another man until he explodes in my mouth. The pastor announces the next part of service, which is the Christening ceremony but I continue until I know Derrick is satisfied.

I rush back into service and make it just in time to witness the best thing life can bring. My heart is filled with so much joy as Kia takes MJ into her arms and makes a vow to love and protect MJ as her own if something ever happens to Michael and me.

Service is officially over and I make my way over to Derrick. As I mentioned before, I want those bitches to know that he is off limits. How could I be so stupid? Especially when I have my entire family on the other side of the sanctuary. So much for me trying to be incognito.

"You should sneak out tonight so that we can finish what we started in the bathroom," Derrick suggests. I know I'm playing with fire and I'll eventually get burnt.

"I'll see what I can do, but you need to get out of here. We have drawn too much attention already." I don't wait for him to respond, I walked toward where Kia and Sean are. I glance toward Michael as he was conversing with some of the church members. He shot an evil look at me. I can see the steam coming from my husband's ears. From that moment, I know the chances of me sneaking out of the house tonight are slim to none.

Michael barely says two words to me while we're having Sunday dinner together with our friends at the steakhouse; however, when we enter our home, he has plenty to say.

Needless to say, nothing is resolved. He fusses… I lie… He goes to bed—on the couch in the basement… Derrick and I have phone sex via FaceTime while MJ sleeps next to me. Ever since we stopped attending our marriage therapy sessions, our communication has dwindled. Deep down inside, I know that everything is my fault. I've made Michael feel as if he was losing his mind about me having affair. Everything my husband has speculated is true. As many times I've said to myself that I'm going to leave Derrick, I've only fooled myself. I don't care that he's been seeing another woman. Nor do I care that treats me like shit. I just need him around. What's even more shocking is that Derrick never questioned the paternity of MJ. I don't think MJ is his; well, according to the timeline, he couldn't be his. A small part of me wishes that Derrick would've asked, at least that would've let me know that he cared.

"How did your appointment go?" I ask Michael as he enters the house. I left work early so that I could come home and cook for my husband. I owe him an apology and doing it over a home cooked meal will hopefully serve me justice.

"It went great. Everything is looking good, at least that's what I was informed," he replies nonchalantly. Something is still bothering him, though. Maybe it's our argument from last night. If it is, this would be a great time to talk about it.

"Look, about last night... I was completely out of line. I should've never said what I said about you not being the man of the house. I shouldn't have disrespected you at church yesterday by entertaining one of my clients. I'm truly sorry. The last thing I would ever want is to make you feel inferior or you have to question my love for you. I will always love you, baby." I mean every word except for the 'client' part, but everything else is true.

"I appreciate it, Ashley." He walks upstairs, but not before putting MJ in his rocker. That is the last I hear from him for the night. When I ask if he wants something to eat, he tells me no. So, I eat alone while MJ sits in his rocker staring at me with those beautiful hazel eyes.

THE NEXT MORNING.

It's early, three o'clock in the morning to be exact, and MJ is crying his lungs out. I was so distracted by Michael's behavior that I forgot to change MJ's diaper before I put him to sleep. No wonder this poor baby is screaming, he's damp and cold. After I change him and finally get him back to sleep, I have a hard time dozing off. Michael doesn't wake up at all and I don't want to bother him. The only person I know that would still be up is Kia. She picked up an extra overnight shift so I decide to call her.

"Bitch, you better be lucky it's slow. What the hell do you want at 3:30 in the morning?" Kia jokes.

"Girl, nothing. MJ woke up crying so I put him back to sleep, and now I can't doze off. How's work?"

"It's slow as hell. I'm actually glad that you called. I wanted to see how you were doing?"

"I'm alright. I have no idea what's going on with Michael, but other than that I'm cool."

"Did you know Derrick was coming to the christening?" she inquires. I was waiting for this question.

"No, I didn't. He made a joke about coming, but I threatened him not to. I apologized to Mike tonight because of that. I should've never went over there to talk to him. I know rumors have been flying around church. I got a Facebook message from Sister Sharon asking me who Derrick was and to remind me that I'm a woman of God first... blah... blah... blah." I embarrassedly admit.

"I wish Sister Sharon would sit her nosey ass down somewhere! She stays in everyone's business; meanwhile, her husband is sleeping with the deacon from Missionary Baptist Church." We both break out into laughter. It isn't a secret that Sister Sharon's husband is bi-sexual. Better yet, he is just completely gay. It's clear as day that he isn't attracted to Sister Sharon.

"Girl, I needed that laugh." I can't keep my composure from laughing so hard. Kia said what everyone was already thinking.

"Are you sure everything is okay, sis? You know you can talk to me about anything," Kia insists.

Her tone turned extremely serious in a matter of seconds. I really want to tell her that I'm still sleeping with Derrick and how I do believe he may have had something to do with my husband being shot. But how stupid would I sound admitting that I believe he had something to do with Michael's accident and still sleeping with him? Kia would never look at me the same, and I would lose the only friend I have in this world.

"No, I'm okay. I didn't want to bother you. I wanted to check up on you. I'm actually about to go back to sleep. I love you, sis."

"I love you too, Ash. If you need anything, you know I got you."

"I got you too," I repeat before I disconnect the call.

I go into the bedroom to try to seduce my husband, but he doesn't budge. Something is totally off with him. I tried to prick and probe the best I could before he went to bed, but he gave me nothing. I even asked if he'd received some bad news from the doctors today, but he said everything was fine. My husband would never lie to me; he's never had a reason to.

I send Sean a text to see if he is up. I don't expect him to respond until hours later but, to my surprise, he texts back right away asking if everything is okay. I advise him that everything is fine; however, I'm concerned about Michael.

"Sis, I'm going to be honest. You need to fix whatever is going on with you and Mike. I don't know if you're having an affair; personally, I don't give a damn. But what I do give a damn about is Mike's happiness and the lack of security he feels being in this marriage. I love you dearly, but my boy is hurt."

I read Sean's text at least thirty times. I don't respond back to him. I make a conscious decision to try to make it up to him these next couple of days. Hopefully, he'll be receptive to my invitations.

***

I wake up within the next two hours to make Michael breakfast in bed. I make French toast, bacon, eggs, cheese grits and biscuits. After he is finished, I run him some hot water so that he can soak before he heads into work. I offer him a deep tissue massage, but he decline because he's running late for work. I drop MJ off at the babysitter and go on about my day. I reschedule all my appointments so that I can get off work earlier than Michael so that he can have dinner waiting for him. I make every attempt to make him happy, but he really doesn't budge. Day after day, night after night, I try everything. Michael just won't open up to me. It has now been a whole week and Michael still seems upset.

"Baby, what's going on with you? This last week you've been so distant. Did I do something wrong?" I ask him over the sirloin steak dinner I prepared for him.

"No, I'm good," he states with absolutely no emotion behind it. I don't press the issue any further. I continue eating and after dinner, Michael showers and goes to bed. He doesn't even kiss me goodnight. I'm not going to lie; my feelings are hurt because I tried to make it my priority to change the dynamic of our relationship.

***

I continue to cater to my husband for the next month, but things have gotten progressively worse, not only in our marriage but in my own personal life. Hour by hour, Michael has become so detached from me and everything I've worked hard for crumbles right before my eyes. My life has taken a complete 180 and I have absolutely no control of it. Maybe it's my karma. Maybe this is God's way of punishing me. Even I wouldn't have ever thought God would be this harsh.

TWENTY-NINE

I received the call that I've been anticipating for the last week, but I didn't expect the results. I knew something was off when they asked me to come into the office instead of providing me with the information over the phone. I quickly get dressed and rush MJ over to Sean's house. Sean and I had spoken, and I told him that doctor had told me I was sterile. The look on his face speaks volumes, and I know he will support me in any decision I make after hearing my results.

What seems like eternity is only a five-minute wait. My stomach bubbles from the time the phone rang until the moment I'm called to the back to hear

CLOSER THAN YOU THINK

my results. I wait another five minutes or so before my regular doctor walks in first. That throws me for a loop because he wasn't the one to administer me the DNA test. Moments later, the therapist follows with the lab technician. I repeatedly ask myself what the hell is going on. I've never known for DNA results to require multiple people in the room.

"Thank you for coming in so soon. We wanted to go over the test results with you in person just in case you have any questions. I figured it would be easier if you had your primary care physician in attendance to help answer any questions, so that's why he's here," the short and hairy technician acknowledges.

My primary doctor nods as he's introduced. Everyone grabs a chair to sit in front of me. I feel as if I'm about to be interrogated. Any time a therapist is in a room, it has to be serious. I learned that from Ashley. What could be worse than me not being the father of my son?

"We received your results, and we've gone over

it a million times to make sure we were right. Um, regrettably, you are not the father of your child. No markers that were tested for paternity matched. In a paternity test, we generally test fifteen markers and in order to be considered the father, all fifteen must match. In your case, the majority of the markers did match; however, not enough to say you're the biological father," he consoles.

"Majority? I don't get it! So that means there's a seventy-five percent chance that my son is mine or what?" I snap.

"Calm down, Michael... let him explain," my doctor interrupts. I sit back down in my chair, overly furious and ready to break everyone's neck in this room.

"The reason the probability test came back inconclusive is because the child has some of your DNA," the tech continues.

"What? I'm so confused right now. You aren't making any damn sense. So you're telling me he's mine… you just said he has some of my DNA!" I yell.

"He does; however, he's not yours. Either this child belongs to your father, or you have a twin brother that you don't know about. And, if that's the case, we need to bring him in for testing as well."

My mouth drops to the floor as I try to process every bit of information that just exploded in my face. I know for a fact that my father is deceased, but I've been in search of my twin brother for years. Is it really possible that my brother is closer than I thought?

"This is a tough situation for you," the therapist interjects. "So if you need to talk, your sessions are free… courtesy of the hospital. Is there anything you want to say? Or perhaps talk about how you're feeling?"

There isn't much for me to say. I'm speechless, torn, heartbroken; destroyed both mentally and physically. How could she do this to me? How could she be so careless? Committing adultery is just wrong, but for you to cheat and not use any protection is completely disrespectful.

"I was separated at birth from my twin brother, we are fraternal twins. I've been in search of him for the last fifteen years. During the course of those years, I learned that my father was deceased. I even visited his grave. My brother, on the other hand, is nowhere to be found. I contacted every foster home where I was told he had resided. I'm totally devastated right now but, on the other hand, it's a possibility that I've found my twin brother."

Everyone is silent and shocked as I speak.

"Is it possible I can have the documentation?" I inquire.

"Sure, is there anything else you would like? Perhaps, speak to someone about how you're feeling?" The therapist replies.

"No, not right now. When I'm ready to talk, I will contact you." I don't give anyone an opportunity to talk or to ask me any more questions as I exit the room as quickly as I came in.

I'm at Sean's house in less than fifteen minutes. Kia is there so I sit them both down and tell them what happened. Kia begins crying while Sean fumes with anger. One would think that he is more upset than I am by the way he's carrying on.

"I think I know who he is!" Kia says in between her soft weeps.

"You knew that bitch was cheating and you didn't say anything, Kia?" Sean curses as he stands directly in her face.

"I... I... tried to tell her to stop. I promise I did, Mike. But she just wouldn't listen to me." Kia places her face in her hands, plunges her head into her lap, and cries uncontrollably. I'm not mad at Kia. I know she loves both Ashley and me. This is a tough predicament to be placed in.

"I'm not mad at you, sis," I say. "How long has this affair been going on?"

"Years, Mike...years. I've told her countless times that she needs to end the affair and how amazing of a man you are. I honestly believe that the guy had something to do with you being shot!"

"Kia, what the fuck! You've been holding all of this in?" Sean scolds. He stands and lounges in the direction of Kia. I grab Sean to help calm his nerves. I thought he was going to hit her at any given moment.

"Kia, why do you think he had something to do with me being shot?" I question, remaining as calm as possible because I need Kia to spill everything she knows about this situation. I sit Sean down and stood directly in front to block him from lounging at Kia a second time.

"His name is Derrick. He didn't know Ashley was married. She lied to him just like she lied to you, Mike. When they were out of town, he must've asked her why he hadn't met any of her friends or family. Ashley hesitated and continued to beat around the bush until he forced her to come clean. He was going to leave her! Instead of Ash letting him leave after she revealed that she was married, she lied and said you were beating her. She told him that was the only reason why she was still married to you. She led him to believe you were a monster and she was afraid of what you would do to her if she left. I know Derrick, and he's a rebel. He grew up in the streets, sold drugs, and has murdered people. It isn't a coincidence that weeks later after she told Derrick that lie, you were shot. I even asked Derrick myself, when I ran into him, if he had something to do with you being shot, and of course he said no."

Sean became hostile and belligerent toward Kia. He lunges at her again. This time, I can't stop him. He shoves Kia into the wall and begins screaming.

"How could you keep this from us? How could you lie to me? I asked you, repeatedly if Ashley was cheating! I even asked if she had something to do with Mike being shot!" Sean howls.

Who could blame him for being upset? She's been hiding a deep secret from not only her husband but from me also. Kia weeps while I stand in shock. MJ is now screaming, possibly because of the commotion. I grab Sean and he slowly steps away from Kia.

"I'll make him a bottle." Kia moves from the wall, swiftly brushes past us, and goes into the kitchen. Luckily, they have extra bottles and milk from babysitting MJ because I'm down to my last bottle. Sean looks at her in utter disgust when she returns to the living room.

"Don't be mad at her. I can understand why she hasn't said anything," I reiterate as I place my hand on Sean's shoulder in hopes to relax him. I figure if he realizes that I'm not as bothered by it then neither should he. I'm almost afraid to leave them alone when I leave.

Even though it takes some time for him to relax, he sits by Kia to console her as she cries. This is emotional for everyone involved. We all truly love each other and respect each other's marriages.

I feed MJ before he falls back to sleep. I want to dig a little deeper and see what I can find about this Derrick.

"Kia, do you know where I can find him?"

"Who?"

"Derrick!"

"He's usually everywhere. Last I heard he was working as a realtor, but I have no idea where. If you want to know where Derrick is, just follow Ashley. She'll lead you right to him."

I hadn't thought about that, but Kia is right. I know Ashley is still sleeping with him; actually, I know every time she sleeps with him because her loving is different.

"I hate to even ask this question, but this has been on my mind since we left MJ's christening…" I start.

"Was that Derrick at the—"

"Yes! That was him!" Kia knew exactly where I was going with my next question, answering before I even finish my question.

"Thanks, Kia. I need a favor from you guys. Please don't let Ashley know anything about what happened. She's about to get a taste of her own medicine."

"She won't hear anything from me. She deserves whatever comes her way. If you need any help, let me know," Kia says, and Sean agrees.

I go home to pack some more bottles and diapers for MJ. I know Ashley goes for lunch around the one o'clock hour, so I sit out in the parking lot of her building. I park my car approximately fifty feet from her car and wait. I keep my routine normal by calling her before she heads out for lunch.

"Hey. baby, what's going on?" I ask after she answers the phone on the first ring. She even sounds thrilled to hear from me.

"Oh, nothing. Probably about to go out for

lunch. I have a late appointment, but I can cancel it and come home if you'd like?" she suggests.

Even though I hate her right now, I do appreciate the effort she's trying to put in to restore our marriage, but it's too late. I'll be filing for a divorce very soon.

"Naw, I'm good. I'll probably hang out with Sean later on anyway," I lie.

"How's my prince doing? Where is he?"

"He's asleep in his crib. I'm going to go check on him in a minute."

"Okay, well, send me a picture of him when he wakes up please?" Ashley begs.

"I sure will. I'll talk to you later."

"I love you, Michael; always have, always will."

"I know. I love you back." I disconnect the call and patiently wait until Ashley comes outside.

Another thirty minutes pass before I decide to

just go home, thinking maybe Ashley decided to eat in the cafeteria instead of going out. As I start the car, she trots to her car. She's wearing a different outfit from the one she had on when she left the house this morning. She gets inside her car, puts on more lipstick, and fixes her hair in the rearview mirror. She starts her car to leave, and I proceed right behind her. I stay at least two or three cars behind her so that I won't be noticed. I peek in my rearview mirror to check on MJ, and he's still sound asleep.

Kia was right. After following Ashley for over an hour, she meets Derrick at a restaurant near a river bay. They share an intimate kiss as he cuffs her ass in the parking lot. She seems to enjoy it thoroughly by bending over to let him slap her ass. I stay in the distance and witness my beloved wife in the arms of another man. Another man who happens to be the father of my son and could possibly be my twin brother. My heart sinks and I can't contain the tears any longer. I look back at MJ, now wide awake and greeting me with the biggest smile that I've ever seen. I am so in love with this baby. It hurts to know that he isn't mine biologically; however, he is still my son. My love hasn't changed and never will.

I change MJ in the backseat and give him some juice. I put a *Mickey Mouse* movie on the iPad attached to the passenger side headrest, and MJ watches intently while I watch Ashley and Derrick from afar. Some time goes by before both Derrick and Ashley exit the restaurant. She climbs into the tinted car with him. It doesn't take a genius to figure out what is going on as the car rocks numerous times and the windows fog up. When she finally exits his car thirty minutes later, she adjusts her dress and fixes her hair. She gets in her car and leaves, yet I waited for Derrick to pull off. I follow him for about ten minutes before he pulls in front of a tall building. He gets out his car with his suit jacket draped over his shoulder. I suddenly remember Kia telling me that he is a realtor, maybe this is where he works. Five minutes later, I get MJ out the car and we head toward the building. I'm not worried about being seen because there are tons of people who enter and exit this building. I search the directory in the lobby, and there are only two realtor firms listed. I take a picture of both names and go on my merry way.

I make it home and immediately become an FBI detective. It doesn't take much to see which firm he works for. I schedule an open house viewing for one of the properties that is listed under his name. It's time to face the man who could possibly be my twin brother. I'm not upset with him that he's sleeping with my wife, even after he knew she and I were actually married. I'm more aroused by the idea of he and I bonding as brothers than wanting to kill him because he could be the reason as to why I was shot.

An email confirms the ten o'clock viewing for tomorrow. Ashley finally calls and asks if I want her to bring dinner home. She claims that she's in the mood for pizza and wings from a local pizzeria down the street from our home.

"Sure, that's fine. Can you get me buffalo wings, though? I didn't care too much for the lemon pepper wings last time." I ask.

"Cool. How many did you want?"

"Ten will suffice; along with the pizza…I should be good." I state.

"Oh, how was lunch? Where did you go?" my curiosity gets the best of me. I just want to know what she's going to say.

"It was fine love, thanks for asking. I ended up grabbing a sandwich from the cafeteria. I was behind on paperwork so I worked through lunch."

All I can do is shake my head while listening to her boldface lie. Had I not followed her, I would've believed every word she just told me. I'm not going to lie; this shit hurts like hell. She's lucky I'm a Christian man because I would've contemplated slashing her throat the moment she walked through the door; however, I'm more thrilled at the idea of getting my revenge. She is about to reap what she's sown.

I keep everything as normal as possible. I kiss her nasty ass on the cheek instead of her lips. I can only imagine what she did with her mouth while she was in the car with Derrick. She showers before she sits down to eat with me at the table. I do everything I can to compress the disgust I have for her. In order for me to do that, I start a small conversation.

"How was work?" I inquire.

"It was great! How was your day? What did MJ and you do today?"

"We didn't do much. I took him into the office for a little while, then we took a stroll through the mall. What's your schedule like tomorrow?"

"Well, I have a couple clients who will be in, in the morning. I have a young lady, who's about fourteen, tried to commit suicide. She was just released from the hospital last week. I can't fathom being sexually abused by my dad while my mom did nothing. Then she had to go to school every day and face bullying. You know they threw her in the garbage can and forced her face into the girls' bathroom stall. Then those bullies had the nerve to record it and put it on social media..." Ashley rumbles on and on.

I pretty much stop listening. I just want to make sure she is busy so when I pay Mr. Derrick a visit, Ashley won't be in the way. That is, if she's telling me the truth about her having a busy day. It's to the point that I can't decipher between her truths and lies.

We finish the night off by watching a movie and putting MJ to bed. Ash wants to make love, but I decline her offer by giving her an excuse of being extremely tired. She knows some of the side effects of the medications that I take daily, and being fatigued is one. Although that reason is by far from the truth, it is legit enough to get her off my back.

***

It is eight a.m. and Ashley is rushing out the door to make it to work. I get up, shower, and get MJ dressed after I feed him. I call Sean to make sure that he is still able to watch MJ for a couple hours for me.

I drive to the location of the open house viewing.

I'm running about five minutes late, which was not in my plan. I wanted to get there before him so I could get a feel of the house just in case a fight breaks out. I pull up in front of the house and I saw a Range Rover parked. A familiar feeling comes over me, one that I can't place my finger on. It's a déjà vu moment but not quite. I get out of the car and am about to ring the doorbell when I am greeted by Derrick. I immediately know that he knows exactly who I am by the startled look on his face.

"What the fuck are you doing here?" he snarls. He becomes aggressive and I am physically and mentally ready for whatever happens next.

THIRTY

No, this bitch ass punk didn't roll up at my place of employment. I don't know what the hell Ashley told him, but I will end his life right here in this house.

"I'm not here for any drama. It's clear that you know who I am," he replies after I get in his face.

"Then why the hell are you here? This is my damn job!" I snap, becoming more hostile by the second. I have my burner in the car, and I am two seconds away from grabbing it from the glove compartment.

"I need to talk to you about something

important," he shares. "Can I come in?"

He must think I'm stupid. There is no way I am letting him into this house. This is a set-up! It isn't a coincidence that Ashley called me this morning, asking where I would be today. That bitch sent her husband to me, and I'm about to deal all this shit.

"You must be ready to die for real today! Look, I don't care that I'm in this suit, I will blow your brains out right here, right now! Now, I'm going to ask you one more time to vacate the premises!"

"Or what?" he says as he stands tall, preparing himself for what is to come.

I must admit, this bitch has balls. Before I am able to put my hands on him, he beats me to the punch; knocking me clean on my ass. I try to stand my ground, but I am unsuccessful as I take every punch he throws. This is a prime example of not judging a book by his cover. He is tougher than I imagined.

Eventually, I am able to get into a stance so that

I can go toe to toe with him before I go out to the car. I give him the best right hook that I have, which sends him to the floor. I stand over him, ready to bash his skull in until I hear him mumble something.

"Speak up, bitch!" I taunt. I really want him to beg for his life because I'm certain that it's about to end here. I will walk away squeaky clean because he came to my place of employment looking for a fight. I had to defend myself!

"I think you're my brother!" he mumbles.

I stand there in a complete state of confusion. How does he know I have a brother that I've never met? I never mentioned this to Ashley, or anyone for that matter! My twin brother and I were separated at birth, but I was told that he died when he was ten. I never found any records of his death. I tried finding him years ago but gave up when no one had any information on him.

"How the fuck you know I have a brother? What the hell are you up to?"

"I think you're my twin brother. That's why I'm here! That's what I came to tell you."

I step away from him as he lay on the hardwood floor. I can tell in his eyes that he is serious. But why would he attack me if that's what he wanted to talk about? I mean, I guess I was harsh as hell and wasn't receptive to hearing anything he had to say.

I continue to stand in shock as he stands to his feet. He keeps his hand over his jaw as he begins to speak.

"I know that you have been sleeping with my wife, but that's not why I'm here. The reason I think you are my brother is because I found out my son isn't my biological son. When I went in to speak to someone at the DNA testing center, they told me that even though MJ isn't mine, he has the majority of my DNA. Either meaning that, he belongs to my dad or that I have a twin brother that I didn't know about. Only my best friend and Ashley knew about my brother. He and I were separated at birth. I tried to find him for over ten years. When I was on that journey searching for my twin, I discovered that my dad was deceased. I even visited his gravesite and retained a copy of his death certificate. My dad was immediately eliminated from that possibility. So I followed Ashley yesterday, which led me straight to you. I followed you guys to the restaurant then I followed you to your office. It didn't take much to find where you worked and to schedule an open house viewing. Now, here I am, standing face to face with a man who could be MJ's dad and my twin brother."

I think my heart stopped beating. As much as I want to hate him, I just can't bring myself to do it. The only thing I know about my family is that my mom was killed in a hit and run and my pops is buried in Texas somewhere. To gather more information from him, I decide to dig a little deeper to see what else he knows about our family heritage.

"Is your mom still alive?" I manage to ask.

"No. She was involved in a hit..."

"...and run." I finish.

"Yes, she was. My dad is buried in Texas," he ends.

It feels like I am about to faint as I watch tears roll down his eyes. If this is true, that he could possibly be my twin brother, then I have to tell him that I tried to have him killed. All of this over some trifling ass bitch who couldn't stay faithful. I feel like shit. I quickly become remorseful. Both of our parents died the exact same way, and if what he's telling me is true about the DNA testing, then it's a strong chance that he could be my brother.

"I'll leave my card with you. Take some time and think this over. Hopefully, you believe me. I hope that you can take a DNA test soon. I'd be happy to go with you," he mentioned as he reaches into his pocket, pulling out his business card. He leaves the card on the table near the door. He exits the house and is on his way to his car before I can stop him.

"Can we take that test today?" I yell from the

front door.

He turns around and glares at me in confusion then walks back toward the house. "Yeah, man. Do you need a ride? I have to pick MJ up along the way." I know this sounds crazy, but I don't decline his invitation. I don't feel him as a threat. A huge part of me knows that he could be my brother and I could be the father of his son. Ashley and I never used protection, and I rarely pulled out. Therefore, if I am the father, I wouldn't be surprised.

I grab my jacket from off the floor and hop in his ride. We make a pit stop by his friend's house to pick up his son. I try to avoid looking at the baby. I'm afraid that I'll see some resemblance and feel like shit. I promised myself that I would never let my child grow up without me. I know what it feels like to grow up without parents and forced into different group homes every year. It's not a good feeling, and I wouldn't wish that on anyone.

We finally make it to the DNA testing center and we have to wait about an hour before we see anyone.

I figure the wait was long because we didn't have an appointment. They swab my mouth then MJ's. They draw blood from me, but I don't see them draw any from the others. They advise us that it will take seven to ten days for the results.

I admire how wonderful of a father Michael is to MJ. He is so attentive and loving, something that I've always desired from my father. I also can't help but notice how beautiful this baby is. I didn't want to admit how much he resembles my baby picture that I still have in my wallet, so I just keep my mouth shut. I also never would've imagined me being in the same room with my enemy and not wanting to kill him. I thought this was going to be difficult for me to handle but surprisingly, it wasn't. If anything, I want to kill Ashley.

We finish up at the clinic, and he drops me off to the house where I thought I was doing a showing for a potential buyer. We don't exchange words, just looks. It's an unspoken communication that we will eventually see each other again once the results were in. He does, however, mention to keep this on the hush from Ashley because he wants revenge, and I agree. Other than that, he has my business card and I have his.

I can't sleep at all that night, contemplating how I will handle Ashley if I find out that this baby is mine and if the man I almost had murdered is my brother. I become nervous at the thought of it all, so much that I become nauseous. Running to the bathroom and praising the porcelain God doesn't help, and my nerves continue to get the best of me.

For the next couple days, I don't eat or sleep, and I continued to ignore all of Ashley's calls. I took a week off from work after possibly learning that I could be a father. I gave my partner all of my potential buyers and told him he can have the profit. I just want to get this whole ordeal over with. We are approaching the sixth day of awaiting the results from the DNA test. I've even called in to see if they were in yet. I have no one to talk to because I got rid of my best friend and there is no way I can tell my girl what is going on. She will be devastated. Now, if I find out that MJ is mine, then that's a horse of a different color. I will deal with it when the time comes. Speaking of which... the clinic number flashes across the screen of my phone.

"Hello, is Derrick Scott available?" a lady asks.

"This is he." I am terrified. My heart is racing and my stomach is in knots.

"Mr. Scott, we have both results from the tests you took. They just came in about fifteen minutes ago."

"Okay, let me hear it," I bluntly respond. There is no need for small talk, let's get right down to business.

"No problem! As far as the test to determine if you are the father of the child in question, there's a 99% chance that you are the father. And hold on, sir... I'm trying to locate the second test results. Ah, here it is! This test is to determine if you and the gentleman in question are brothers, and the result is conclusive. Congratulations, not only have you found your brother, but you are going to be a..."

I disconnect the call on that happy ass representative and immediately start crying. I honestly don't know if this is tears of joy or tears of sorrow. All these years I've wanted to find my brother, but I never would've thought I would find him like this. Then that innocent baby! How could she do that to him or her husband? How could she lie to me about her husband beating her? How could I be so stupid and believe that bitch? These are the questions that continue to play over and over in my head.

After about ten minutes or so, I search for Michael's number, but he beats me to the punch and calls me first.

"Hello, is this Derrick?" Michael questions. It's quite obvious that he has been crying too. I can hear the tremble in his voice.

"Yes, this is your brother," I force myself to say

without breaking down, but the fact that I now know he's my brother got the best of me and I couldn't hold it in any longer. I start weeping and so does Michael.

"Is it okay if I stop by?" he asks after our sobs.

"Sure." I give him my address and wait for him to show up. My anticipation grows as I wait for him to pull up in front of my house. Although it only takes twenty minutes, it feels like an eternity. This is the moment I have only dreamed of, I'm about to meet my twin brother. It doesn't matter that I already met him a week ago, this time it is official. Not only is my brother still alive, I'm also a dad.

He pulls into my driveway but he doesn't have MJ with him. I was expecting to see him too, but maybe Michael isn't ready for that yet. I definitely understand as to why he opted out of bringing my son. I open the door and wait for him to exit his car. This is the most vulnerable I've ever been. I'm emotional and regretful all mixed up in one.

He greets me with a strong embrace that lasts for

a couple of minutes. All the hatred and animosity I've had toward him wholly dissipates. This is the reunion I prayed for, and now it's finally here.

We finally separate from our embrace and I invite him inside my house. I ask him if he wants something to drink and he suggests a bottle of water. Neither of us knows where to start, we're both mute. One thing about me is if I feel I need to get something off my chest, I will do; whether it's right or wrong. It's been tugging at my heart knowing that I am the reason he still walks with a slight limp and still has therapy twice a week. And there is no way I can build a relationship with my brother without informing him of my faults.

"There's something I need to tell you. You aren't going to like this one bit, but I can't continue to keep it bottled in."

"I think I know what you're about to say, but go ahead and tell me," he replies.

"I'm the reason you were shot!" I hurry it along.

333

I'm not afraid of him, but I am afraid of what could come next as far as us building a brotherhood. I continue.

"Trust me, if I could do it all over again, I would. Ashley lied. She lied about being married, she lied about you beating her; she lied about everything. When I confronted her and she finally admitted that she was married, I was going to leave her. I don't come second to no man, period! I guess she felt the need to let me know that she was in an abusive relationship and she was afraid to leave, so that I wouldn't leave her. She played us both. All this time I thought you were kicking her ass. It never dawned on me that I'd never seen any bruises on her. But me being the man and the protector that I am, I felt it was my duty to get rid of you so that she and I could be happy together. So an old friend of mine and I followed you and studied your daily routine. That's why we knew you were going to be at the gym that night. We knew that there would be no cameras in the parking lot and that would be the perfect opportunity to hurt you. I swear, sincerely, I apologize. I know it may not mean anything to you, but I truly can't express to you enough how remorseful I feel right now," I express wholeheartedly.

Michael looks me dead in the eye. I can't tell if he is infuriated or shocked. I just pray he doesn't react the way I would've reacted if another man told me he was the reason I was almost killed. If he decides to try anything crazy, unfortunately, I will have to end his life for real this time.

"The trips…" he says.

"Huh? Trips?" I repeat, still confused.

"The elaborate trips to the Bahamas, Jamaica… were you with her?"

"Yes! I paid for those trips. I love to travel, so I brought her along with me," I reveal to him. It doesn't take a rocket scientist to know that she lied to him about who she was going on these trips with or why she was even going.

335

"How long have you and her been sleeping together?" he asks after processing everything I've told him thus far.

"For almost three years," I tell him. I knew he is devastated. You can see it all over his face. I want to comfort him, but I know this isn't the right time to do so. I can't imagine the way he feels. If this burden is heavy on me, I know it has to be ten times heavier on him.

"I forgive you." Michael stares at me and repeats it again, "I forgive you, my brother."

The words are like music to my ears. It takes a real man to forgive another man for basically destroying his life. Although, his wife ultimately is the reason, I take full responsibility in it too. I give him another hug, and we decide to move forward. We leave it in the past and start brainstorming on how we will repay Ashley for what she's done.

"What do you have in mind?" I question Michael to get even.

"Destroying everything she's worked hard for."

"Well, I'm down for that. I just need to know how dirty you are willing to get." I hint.

"As dirty as necessary. However, I'm not trying to go to jail or kill the girl either," he firmly counters.

"I wasn't thinking of killing her." I laugh. "But I know just the thing to do. I just need to know if you're in it 100%. If you're not, then it will not work."

"I'm all in. I'm so done with her. I've already filed for a divorce, and she will be served soon!"

"Alright… listen…"

THIRTY-ONE

After receiving those test results, it broke me down to the point I was on my knees asking God if he ever loved me. I was good to this woman! I was the kind of man every woman prayed for. My good looks were an extra bonus. My heart was pure and fragile, and Ashley took advantage of it. Even though MJ isn't biologically my son, he is still my blood; he's my nephew. I didn't think things could get any worse until Derrick revealed his secret; he was the one who had me shot. I could've died because of Ashley's whore-ish behavior. Had she kept the vow she made to not only God but to me, we wouldn't be in the predicament. But it's too late—it's time that she lay in the messy bed that she has made.

I eagerly listen as Derrick shares his plan of how we are going to get Ashley back. I think I'm more excited than a kid on Christmas morning. His plan is amazing, and I am all in for it. Ashley is a licensed therapist and it is against policy for her to have any sexual contact with her patients. Derrick told me he was her patient first, that's how their affair began. We decide to plant a hidden camera in her office when he goes to see her in a couple days. We agree to keep everything as normal as possible so that Ashley doesn't become suspicious. I thought I would backpedal at the idea of destroying my wife but to my surprise, I have no remorse. I am overly excited to find my brother and that matters the most to me.

The next day after work, I send Derrick a text asking if he wants to see MJ, and he replies, 'More than anything'. I pick MJ up from the babysitter and go to Derrick's home. It hurts me to know that my son is now my nephew. I try to look at the bright side of things, knowing that I will still be part of his life. I'm actually glad that everything happened now when MJ is young, so he doesn't understand what is going on. When the time comes and he questions why his mom and I got a divorce and why he's named after me and not Derrick, I will let Ashley handle it.

"I was thinking about something else, you know, to destroy Ashley," Derrick mentions as he towers over me as he rocks MJ to sleep.

"Thinking about what?" I wonder. What else could we possibly do to destroy Ashley? I mean, within the next two weeks, she will lose her license and not be able to practice anymore once the video gets sent to the National Association of Social Workers.

"Ashley has some bricks stored somewhere in your house. She could get major jail time if she's caught with it." He smirks.

I smirk too. If she's in jail, she can't fight the divorce. It will automatically be granted if she's incarcerated. So I am already in love with this plan. I smile and advised him to do whatever it takes to bring her ass down.

"I'm down with everything, but under one condition only…" I bargain.

"What's that?"

"That MJ name remains the same. If he ever asks, just let him know that you named him after me, please," I humbly plead.

"Done! I have no intentions of changing his name. We are all family. He will have two dads, something that you and I never had. MJ is blessed and will forever be blessed, as long as we both agree to be his father."

"Deal!"

Days pass, and Derrick and I become closer by the minute. I am well aware of the moment he goes into Ashley's office to make love to her. He informed me as he arrived. After he is done and waits for Ashley to come out of the bathroom to freshen herself up, he removes the camera from her shelf and places it in his bag. He scatters before she returns. I've become numb to my feelings for Ashley. I even made love to her the night before as if nothing was bothering me. Derrick is right, you have to treat a whore like a whore and unfortunately, she wears the "whore" crown proudly. Every day after, I've waited for Ashley to come home distraught that she had to go before her board and every day, she comes home happier than the day before.

M: *Did you send the video off yet? She hasn't gotten fired or at least she hasn't mentioned it yet?* I text Derrick a couple days after the incident in her office. I'm worried that Derrick is retracting on our plans.

D: *Yeah, I sent it via email to them yesterday. I was notified that it was opened and read early this morning, so she should be called into a meeting very soon. Don't worry, bro,* he confirms.

M: *I'm not. I'm just ready for her to go down. Just make sure you keep everything as normal as possible. When she calls you crying, just act shocked and hurt by it,* I reply.

"I got it!"

A couple more days go by before Ashley finally comes home crying like someone died. I already knew it was coming because she reached out to Derrick letting him know that someone recorded their love-making session. Derrick said he pretended to be angry and distraught by the whole ordeal. She even asked what she should tell me when she got home. I found that to be hilarious that she would ask another man what he thought would be ideal to tell me, her husband. So I was a bit curious to see what excuse she was going to give me to why she lost her license and her job.

"Oh my God, honey, what's wrong? What happened?" I pretend to be concerned.

"I lost my job today, nor can I practice anymore. My life is ruined," she heavily weeps.

"Wait, what? You lost your license? How did that happen?" I feign shock.

"Someone must have switched my charts and I misdiagnosed an individual with the wrong medications. They had an allergic reaction and died."

This story would've almost been believable had I not known that therapists aren't allowed to prescribe medications.

"Damn baby, I'm so sorry. Everything is going to be okay. I promise," I reassure as I grab her to console her. She cries in my arms, and I continue to remind her that everything is going to be okay. Eventually, she goes upstairs to get some rest. I run her some hot water so that perhaps she will relax. I really give zero fucks about how she feels but I have to play the nurturing husband role.

I send my brother a text telling him job well done. He instantly replies with a smiley face emoji. The connection Derrick and I have is amazing. We see eye to eye on pretty much everything. Even though he tried to kill me, it's the will of God in me that forgave him. Hell, I even forgive Ashley for what she's done to me. She's completely ruined my life. Everything I dreamt of or desired, she destroyed. I've always desired to have a family, a wife and children. Ashley stripped that dream from me. In a weird way, I'm grateful for her infidelity. Because of her, my life is now complete.

I wait until Ashley is sound asleep, and I give Sean a call.

"Hey, is it okay for me to stop by. I have some shit to tell you that's going to blow your mind."

"Yeah, come on. Just make sure you bring my nephew with you. I miss little man already." He utters. I'm convinced that Sean is more eager to see my son than he wants to see me. I want to keep him abreast of what is going on. He has no clue that Derrick is my brother but when he hears about what happened, he's going to flip.

"Welcome, come on inside. Give me my nephew first," he says as he pretty much snatches MJ from my arms. MJ loves his uncle Sean. His chubby face smiles as soon he lays eyes on Sean as we enter the door.

"Man, do I have some mess to tell you. These last couple of weeks have been hectic," I begin as I remove my jacket. Sean removes MJ's sweater as we head to his basement. I didn't see Kia, so I assumed she is at work. I grab a water from the counter and follow closely behind Sean. It warms my heart to see how much Sean loves my nephew.

"Alright, tell me what's been going on with you? I haven't heard from you in a couple days. I thought you were upset with me about what I said the last time we spoke. You know I didn't mean any harm by it. You're like my brother, so I'm going to always look out for you."

"Sean, I appreciate that. But no, I wasn't upset about what you said. Actually, you were right about her. That's what I came over here to talk to you about. I need for you to get comfortable because what I'm about to tell you will blow your socks off." I grimace. Just the idea of Ashley makes my stomach turn.

"Wait, this is serious huh? What the hell happened?" Sean explodes, making MJ uncomfortable. Sean starts bouncing him on his knee while rubbing his back. He chants, "It's okay, nephew, Daddy made me a little nervous."

"He's my nephew!" I correct Sean.

"Huh? What the hell are you talking about?"

"MJ isn't my son, he's my nephew. The guy Ashley has been having an affair with is the father of MJ," I explain.

"I'm so confused. The only way he can be your nephew is if the guy is your brother. Even still, we haven't been successful in finding him."

I don't utter a single word as I stare directly at him until he understands what he just said. His eyes widen, and his mouth drops to the floor.

"Oh shit! You mean to tell me that the dude Ashley has been fucking is your twin? Are you freaking kidding me?" Sean asks in astonishment.

"Regrettably, yes." I sigh.

"Oh my God! That bitch! How did you find all of this out?"

"We took a DNA test. That's when I found out that he was my brother and that MJ is his son."

"Yo, wait, I'm so confused. Let's start from the beginning. I'm sorry, I'm just trying to understand this whole crazy-ass fiasco. So how did you two get to the point where you both decided to take a DNA test?" Sean still seems perplexed about everything.

"I followed Ashley during lunch. She met up with him. She led me right to him. Earlier that day, I got the results back that MJ wasn't mine, so that's why I stalked her. I wanted to see who this other guy was. When I finally met up with him, I told him and he agreed to take a DNA test."

"I'm sorry, Mike. I haven't met a man who agrees to take a DNA test just because some man approaches him and asks him to. There's more to this story than what you are telling."

MJ starts to doze off which I knew he would. The sitter told me he hasn't taken a nap all day so I knew it would be only a matter of time before he would be out.

Sean has a blank stare on his face as he listens to my retelling of these traumatic events. I try my best to not laugh, but his facial expressions are killing me.

"I want to meet your brother, and kick his ass for trying to murder you." Sean acknowledges and chuckles.

"You will, in due time."

"Is there anything else you need to tell me about this trifling ass bitch? I'm sorry, but I'm done with her ass. She's no longer welcome in my house. I hope you leave her ass alone. I'm always going to support you in whatever you decide to do, but I pray one of your decisions is to disown this marriage. There's no coming back from that," Sean vents.

I hate to agree, but he is right. When I made a vow to love Ashley for better or for worse, I meant it. Even though I still love her, I am no longer in love with her. I probably would've tried to work it out, but what she's done is irreparable.

"It's cool. I'm pretty much over Ashley's antics. She just lost her job and her license today. Apparently, someone switched her charts and she administered the wrong drugs to the wrong patient, and the patient died. So, it's a good feeling watching everything she worked hard for, crumble." There is no way I am going to tell Sean how Derrick and I plotted against her. I did not want to risk the chance of Sean slipping up and mentioning it to Kia. Kia's mouth runs like water and she despises Ashley. She could tell her out of spite.

"That's what she gets. I have no remorse. Now kick her ass out of your house," Sean chuckles, even though I know he is extremely serious. If I could, I would put her ass out but the house is in her name, so she can have it. I've already gotten approved for a townhome a couple miles from where Derrick resides. I'll be renting, but I'm content with that until

I find something permanent.

"Naw, she can have the home. I'm about to move out anyway. I filed for divorce. I'm just waiting for her to get served. My attorney goes before the judge sometime this week. I'll be officially done with her within the next couple months." I gloat with glee.

"Good! I'll take a couple days off work to help you pack if you want?"

"That'll be cool. Well, let me get back home and pretend to care about what happened to Ashley today," I say sarcastically while reaching for my sleeping prince.

"Don't change the love you have for MJ. He's innocent," Sean adds his input.

"My love will never change, it's unwavering and everlasting. Isn't that right MJ?" I whisper into my nephew's ear. He will always be my son. I will eventually be able to tolerate MJ calling Derrick *dad* and calling me *uncle*.

"Salute to you!" Sean and I shake up right before I leave his home. I strap MJ into his car seat and decide to drive around to collect my thoughts. The tears begin to fall as I reminisce on the first time I held MJ and the first time I laid eyes on Ashley. I honestly thought she and I would be forever. Never in a million years that I would see the ending to a beautiful story. My peace comes from knowing that I did everything I was supposed to do in our marriage, and I did the best I could. Now, I have to learn how to live without her and build a relationship with my brother.

THIRTY-TWO

Ashley has fallen into a deep depression after losing her license and her practice. Word traveled quickly as rumors spread across the city about her sleeping with her patients. I was in the grocery store when I overheard two women gossiping about it. I smiled and patted myself on the back. But it isn't over. Michael and I have one more in us. This will eventually be the demise of Ashley. After telling him that his wife stored an illegal substance for me in his home without his knowledge, he was on board to do whatever it took to bring her down. Granted, we both knew it wasn't our place to bring havoc into her life, but it feels good to sit back and watch.

"Hey, what's going on?" I ask Ashley after she answers her cell phone on the first ring. I'm about to put my next plan into motion.

"Nothing much, just laying here with MJ. How are you?"

"I'm good. I've been thinking about us lately, and I've concluded that we should go our separate ways. I mean, I'm seeing another woman now and your husband is back home. So it's best that we end what we have going on. I think you're an amazing woman, but just not the woman for me."

"Wow, really? After all we've been through and this is how you want to end it? I thought you loved me?" she whines.

"I do, but I'm just not in love with you. There's a big difference. So let's just end the shit now!"

"It's not over until I say it's over!" she demands.

"Oh, it's over. It was over the day you lied about your husband being abusive. Yeah, I've done some research. That man ain't never put his hands on you. You are a lying bitch, and that's all you will ever be!" I snap.

"Fuck you! You ain't shit! Your sorry ass mother should've aborted your pussy ass. I would've given you away too if I was her!"

Any other time, I would've driven to the bitch's house and choked her up had she said anything about my mother, but this time is different. Her words don't bother me anymore because I know I have the upper hand.

"That's fine, you can feel how you want. You need to bring my duffle bag that you have stashed at your house to me. Then we can part ways!"

"You have got to be out of your rabbit ass mind if you think I'm going to get up with MJ and bring you your drugs. I should sell it and pocket the profit," she threatens.

"If you do that, I will personally tell Michael about us. I will tell him the real reason you lost your job. I will show him every nude picture you've sent me. I will even show him our sex tape, and then I will kill you. So try me if you want to, bitch. I don't have shit to lose, but you do!" I rebut.

"You are a piece of shit, you know that!" she yells.

"Let me know when you're on the way. I expect my merchandise within the next hour!"

"I have my son with me! I don't want to drive with him and your drugs in my damn car!" she scolds.

"I don't care! Just drive the damn speed limit and be here within the next hour, like I said. Text me when you're on the way."

She disconnects the call and I patiently wait until I receive a text saying that she is on her way. I FaceTime her to make sure she isn't lying. I even have her pull over so that I can verify that my duffle bag is in her trunk.

"Alright, see you soon."

***

"Seton County Police Department, this is Linda speaking, how may I direct your call?"

"Hi, I want to report a vehicle that's headed southbound on Wheeling Highway. It's a dark blue, 2017 BMW, license plate number; 5148844. The female who's driving the car is carrying approximately forty pounds of crack cocaine."

"Are you sure about this, sir? Is this a prank?" the dispatcher asks in curiosity. It's evident that they aren't used to people tipping others off.

"I'm very sure. You guys are trying to cut down on drug dealers, right? Well, I'm handing you one on a silver platter!"

"We have an officer on it right now. Do you care to provide your name?"

"Hell no! Have a good day!"

I disconnect the burner cell then pick up my phone to text Michael to let him know everything is a go.

D: It's handle. No more worries.

M: "Good! This is music to my ears. Oh, did you want to get together this weekend? My best friend, Sean and I were thinking about hitting up a bar in town."

D: "That sounds like a plan. Just let me know when and where, I'll be there. If it's cool, I would like to bring my girl along."

M: "No, please, bring her. I would love to meet her."

Things are already looking brighter. I came clean to my girl about everything, and to my surprise, she was receptive. I know she is hurt; however, she loves me and is willing to do what it takes to better our relationship. She is excited to meet MJ and my twin brother, Michael. I made a vow to her that I will do my best to make her happy and that she didn't have to worry about any outside drama anymore. She deserves the world and I was about to give it to her. I know she isn't anything like Ashley. I've already met her family and friends. I've been to her house, her job, her church, etc. She is an open book. She doesn't have any children but wants to someday. If everything goes according to plan, she will be my wife next year and will bear my children shortly after. My career has taken off, I'm done with the drug game, and I am done with Ashley's lying ass. My life is fabulous.

THIRTY-THREE

Ashley

"Shit, the fucking cops!" I whisper aloud. I don't know why they stopped me. I wasn't speeding at all. I peek at MJ in the rearview mirror to make sure he's properly secured. I smile at him and he smiles back. My stomach is turning as I try my best to remain calm. I don't want the cops to divert their attention to my trunk where Derrick's drugs are.

"Ma'am, could you step out of your car please?" the officer asks of me.

"I'm sorry, why?"

"Ma'am, please step out of your car, now!"

Four police cars pull up behind the officer's

cruiser. A K-9 unit pulls in front of my car.

"I'm not getting out of my car until you tell me why? I wasn't speeding. My son and I are properly strapped in and all my lights are working just fine. Why did you pull me over?" I maintain my composure even though I am boiling on the inside. Plus, I don't want to startle MJ either.

"We just received a tip, and we need for you to exit your vehicle," the middle-aged, Caucasian man hollers.

MJ becomes agitated and begins to whine, so I get out of the car. The two officers quickly grab me and pull me over to the side of the curb. They aren't aggressive but they aren't gentle either. A female officer removes MJ from the back seat of my car.

"Where are you going with my child?" I yell at her.

"Nowhere ma'am, I'm bringing the child near you."

She's true to her word. She doesn't let me hold him but she stands near me so that I can assist in keeping MJ relaxed. He is already beginning to cry and fuss.

The K-9 unit and six officers search my car. Another female officer was called to the scene. I'm not a dummy, I know Derrick tipped me off, but I don't know why he would do that. I mean, if he wanted to destroy me, all he has to do is send Michael everything about our affair. So maybe he didn't tell on me. Maybe, his phone is tapped...yeah, that's it!

"Pop the trunk!" one of the officer's yell. I immediately put my head down because I know what they are going to find.

"It's here! Lock her up!" another officer demands.

The same two officers lift me up and the female cop handcuffs me while the other continues to hold my baby. MJ is hysterical and so am I. I fight as hard as I can to no avail. I keep asking them what is going to happen to my son, but no one answers me. Derrick has at least three bricks of coke in that bag. That's twenty plus years for me.

They throw me in the hard-ass backseat as I attentively wait to hear what is going to happen next. I pray for God to get me out of this situation, but it seems the harder I pray, the deeper I dig a hole for myself. I just want to hold my son and go home. I keep trying to explain to the officers that the drugs don't belong to me, but no one wants to hear my side of the story. After twenty minutes of them completely destroying my car, two officers enter the car that I am sitting in and drive away.

"What about my son? I don't want to leave without him!" I grimace.

"Ma'am, he's coming down to the station. He's okay. Do you have someone to come and pick him up?" the officer questions.

"Yes, my husband. Please call him as soon as we get there. My son doesn't need to be around this bullshit!"

We finally pull into the station, and I am escorted to get processed. I can hear MJ in the far distance. I question another officer about whether or not my husband can pick up my son and hopefully bail me out. That's when I am told that I won't be awarded bail and that I will go before a judge in two days. I go completely ballistic. There is no way I am going to sit inside this dirty ass jail for two nights.

"So you mean to tell me that I can't post bail? Are you kidding me? These aren't my drugs. They belong to Derrick Scott. He told me to hold it for him! Don't you see that? I've never been arrested in my life, so why now? I've been framed!" I scream.

Every officer that I try to explain my story to is still ignoring me. I'm finally escorted to the area where my mugshot is taken. I am so humiliated; all I can do is cry. They take my fingerprints and process my information into the system. I am officially a criminal. What is more upsetting is that no one asked me where I got the drugs? I would have at least thought that would be the first question that was asked.

I have to remove all my jewelry and turn it over to the booking officer. They have my cell phone and my purse. They even have my diaper bag for MJ. I didn't think I could be more humiliated until they take me inside a small room where I am asked to remove all of my clothes. I fall to my knees and ball up into a fetal position. I cry so hard. I've never experienced anything like this. I shouldn't be here, I should be at home with my family.

My tears don't faze any of the female officers because one of them lifts me up and helps me get undressed. If I didn't know any better, I would've thought she enjoyed watching and helping me remove my clothes. The other female officer puts a pair of latex gloves on and begins to fondle every part of my body.

"Are you on your cycle?" She questions before she inserts two fingers into my vagina. She then inserts those same two fingers into my rectum. I am glad that I just had a bowel movement before I left the house because she had residue on her gloves. Even though I am in a little pain from her being extremely rough, I chuckle as the look of disgust covers her face after she removes the gloves from her hands.

"Put your clothes back on, bitch!" the short, stubby officer orders. I do as I am told and still wear the same smirk on my face as when she discovered the shit residue on her gloves. I know I'm getting under her skin, that's why she pushes me to the ground.

"Keep playing with me, bitch! I'll make your night a living hell!" the officer howls with intimidation.

I keep my cool because I don't want any of these manly ass bitches coming into my cell, trying to eat me out. But I stay ready for war.

I'm walked back to a cell where I ask if I can make a phone call. One of the officers is generous enough to allow me to use the phone. I actually make four calls: one to Michael, Derrick, Kia, and Sean. No one answers their phone. Because I didn't get an answer, they tell me I can try again in about an hour.

"What about my son? Where is he?" I ask the officers that are sitting in front of me. One of them tells me that he was just picked up by my husband.

"Why the fuck no one came and got me? I need to see him!"

"Ma'am, you aren't allowed any visitors. Besides, you were in the back being processed!"

"He didn't ask to even see me? He didn't try to stay?"

"No, ma'am, he didn't. In an hour, you can try to call him back. In the meantime, please shut the hell up!" the officer barks as the rest of his friends laugh at his smart-ass remark.

I sit against the wall and lay down. I continue to sob until I doze off. A couple hours have gone by when someone wakes me up so that I can try to contact someone. Once again, I sneak and make four more calls to the exact same people. No one answers! I make one last attempt before one of the guards disconnects the call.

"That's it! You can try again in the morning. It's lights out!"

I march right back to my cell and cry myself to sleep once again.

THE NEXT MORNING

The next morning took forever to get here. I barely slept last night. I was cold and uncomfortable. I shared a cell with six other individuals, and there was only one stall in the middle of the cell. They gave us a dry ass bologna sandwich that looked as if it was made last week and left on the counter. The bread was hard and the meat was an orange-pinkish color. The only thing that was decent was the bottled water. They gave us breakfast, which was some fruits and juice. We were able to shower and were provided a change of clothing. The clothes don't properly cling to my figure, but at least they are clean.

"Has anyone been here to see me yet?" I ask no one in particular. I'm loud enough for everyone in the precinct to hear me.

Everyone in unison says, "No."

"Well, can I try to make a phone call? I haven't gotten in contact with anyone, and I need a lawyer."

"One can be appointed to you if you don't have one," someone responds.

"I don't need any of y'all fake ass attorneys. My husband will get me one. I just need to talk to him!" It's clear that I'm not trying to make any friends, everyone in here hates my guts. The arresting officer slides the phone toward me, but again, no one answers! I am becoming enraged. How could no one try to come down to the station and see what is going on. There's no telling what they told my husband; he probably is disappointed in me. I would think, after all we've been through, he would still have my back.

He knows me. He knows that I wouldn't have anything to do with drugs. I don't even take aspirin when I'm sick.

Another day and night go by and I'm not able to contact anyone. Nobody has tried to come see me or find out what the hell is going on. I get on my knees and start praying, asking God to grant me a favor. God knows I'm innocent, but I need for the judge to see that as well.

Dear God,

What have I done to deserve this? I'm a good person. I know I've done some things that weren't pleasing to you, but I don't deserve any of this. I come to you as humble as I know how, to ask that you grant me a favor as I appear in front of the judge tomorrow. I know that you are sovereign and you are strong. However, I am not. I am weak and at your mercy, Father. Somewhere down the line, my focus was blurred and I've disappointed you in every way imaginable. Father, I apologized for everything I've done that shamed you and my family. I know favor rests on me, but only if I seek you. I will start and continue to seek you oh God. Even if favor is not granted for me, I will still seek you. You deserve all the praise. I know you would not allow any circumstances to hold me back for the plan you have for my life, and I know this isn't the plan you have designed for me. I'm going to trust that everything will work out. My God, I love you and thank you for being merciful and faithful even though I'm not deserving of your grace.

I end my prayer and go to bed confident that things will work in my favor. There is no way I'm going to jail tomorrow. I try to sleep, but I toss and turn all night long. Before I know it, the sun is peeking through the glass window. I shower when it is my time and put on the same clothes I had on the day I was arrested. I'm grateful that they were washed. I am greeted by another individual who gives me a manila envelope.

"You have been officially served!" He walks right out of the precinct without another word.

"Served? Wait, come back!" I try to stop him but am pulled back by the cop who is standing near me. I carefully open the envelope and see divorce papers. My dear husband filed for a divorce. I don't get a chance to read through the paperwork because I have to appear in court in thirty minutes. My heart sinks to the pit of my stomach. I don't have much time to process what is happening because I am handcuffed again and ride in silence to the courthouse that is near the precinct. As soon as I walk into the courtroom, I am taken aback to what I see. There is Michael and Derrick sitting next to each other. It is then I know that I was set up my Derrick, I just didn't think Michael would be in cahoots with him. As soon as I am uncuffed, I lunge directly at the them but am immediately tackle down by an officer who stands near the back of the courtroom. Neither Derrick or Michael flinch but both greet me with the same evil ass grin. It's almost scary how much they look alike, so much that they could be related. I hate the both of them. It's because of them that I'm in this predicament now.

"It was his drugs, Your Honor! These bitches set me up!" I continue to yell throughout the courtroom.

The judge bangs his gavel against his desk repeatedly, chanting "Order in the court", but I ignore it. I continue my rant while the judge orders me to be held in contempt and requests a continuation. I am dragged out of the courtroom by the cops who walked me in.

"Both of you bitches are going to pay for this! Fuck both of you!" I howl as the judge advise the officers to get me out of the room.

Both Derrick and Michael walk out laughing and giggling while I am restrained. I am taken back to the squad car and placed in the backseat. I watch in astonishment as Kia holds MJ, giving him right to Derrick as she meets them coming out of the courthouse. I had no idea my best friend was in on this bullshit. Simultaneously, we all lock eyes on each other. Kia blows a kiss at me while Derrick smirks. Michael is emotionally wounded, and I know it's because of me. He wears his pain on his sleeves.

My car finally starts to drive off as I hold my head down. That is the last time I'll ever lay eyes on them. The life that I once had, is now extinct.

the
End

Follow Jaycee

Amazon

Facebook

READ Jaycee

Lust, Lies, and Deadly Secrets

Lust, Lies, and Deadly Secrets Book II

CPSIA information can be obtained
at www.ICGtesting.com
Printed in the USA
FSHW022024210219
55859FS

9 781793 814517